when life gives you sunsets

THE ENERGY SERIES
BOOK 2

BROOKELYN MOSLEY

85 MEDIA LLC

When Life Gives You Sunsets

Copyright © 2023 by Brookelyn Mosley

All rights reserved.

No part of this book may be reproduced in any form or by any electronic or mechanical means, including information storage and retrieval systems, without written permission from the author, except for the use of brief quotations in a book review.

contents

ENVY

Ready or Not

So This is Love

Home Before Midnight

GLUTTONY

When Luke Met Juliette

Short Stories

Just Friends

Chateau Luxure

Lena's Ex-File

Dream Boss

Unsilent Knight

Twice In Love

Home For Christmas

message from the author

Thank you for your purchase of *When Life Gives You Sunsets*. This story serves as book two in The Energy Series. Like book one, *When Luke Met Juliette*, *When Life Gives You Sunsets* is a standalone as well. So, if this is your first-time hearing of The Energy Series, you can start with *When Life Gives You Sunsets* and work your way back to *When Luke Met Juliette* if you choose.

This story, like many of the stories in my catalog, contains sexually explicit content and mild profanity. Because this story has a character who is a widower, vivid scenes portraying grief and capturing said character grieving the death of a spouse are present throughout this story.

With all that said, enjoy *When Life Gives You Sunsets*. It is truly a story I believe has changed me as a writer and as a person, too. I pray you experience the same.

Bon voyage!

Love,
BK

acknowledgments

A loving thank you to my amazing husband who is without a doubt one of my biggest supporters. Your support is worth its weight in gold. A special thank you to my reading family and early supporters of my work. I'm sure you've noticed the changes; you've even commented on it. I thank you for sticking beside me and growing with me. You all have embraced my brand of writing and I'm beyond appreciative of it. Shout out to the readers who have reached out to me to share your thoughts regarding my books. I thank you for keeping me motivated and excited to create new projects for you. When I write, I keep you in mind. Thank you for your support. It's my soul food. And a special thank you to Hawaii. Yes, Hawaii. Without that island, this story would be so incomplete.

"Whew, God ... I've seen what you've done for others."

CLARKE ALI - *WHEN LUKE MET JULIETTE*

one

NEW YORK, NEW YORK SATURDAY,
JULY 8, 2023...

CLARKE

I JUST COULDN'T LOOK AWAY. COULDN'T blink either. I couldn't do anything except for stare.

Laughter and conversation floated in one ear and out the other, colored by smooth background music.

I stood frozen in the middle of two large doors, staring straight ahead of me for so long my eyes were watering.

Or was I crying?

Was I about to cry over this?

I mean... I could.

My watering eyes followed my friend Esme as she strutted farther into the party hall.

She glanced to her right, then did a half turn on her designer heels to find me standing at the entrance, frozen where I stood.

"Clarke," she called, stopping in place. "Why are you just stuck there?"

Because I couldn't believe what I was seeing in that packed room of well-dressed men and women.

Old school R&B bounced off the party hall's decorated walls. A giant gray metal fan stood tall near the entrance feet away from me. Its metal blades propelled clockwise, blowing hot air throughout the rented space. The blue and gold balloons of different hues swayed with that air.

Blue foil balloon letters spelled out a name along the wall behind an expansive table straight ahead. Gifts beautifully wrapped in blue and ranging in all sizes, crowded the table's legs on both ends.

A room full of blue and gold, but all I could see was red.

"Clarke," Esme called once more. She glanced around the room, moving her blue gift bag off one arm and onto the other as she neared me again. "Girl, *what* is going on?"

"That's..." I shook my head in disbelief. "Esme, that's *him*."

Her button nose scrunched up like it usually did when something confused her. "Him, *who*?"

"Nico."

She blinked twice. "What?"

That was a fair reaction. Because I couldn't believe what I was saying either.

I shifted my eyes off her and pointed them in Nico's direction, and she turned again to follow my line of sight.

A moment of pause followed by a loud gasp before she shouted, "Oh!"

"Right?"

Esme and I had just slid into our seats in the ride share vehicle she ordered on an app, and I was showing her a photo of my new boyfriend on my phone.

She'd grown tired of me bragging about this guy I met at a Jamaican restaurant in Manhattan two months ago and asked if I had a picture of us together so she could finally put a face to his name. She was annoyed every time I told her the story of how the servers took forever to give me my takeout order of oxtail and rice with peas, and how he used his charismatic charm to get them to speed things up, so I'd walk out of there with my food still hot. He'd later reveal that he was friends with the owner, but his game was original, and I couldn't refuse giving him my number.

"He looks like that actor from the movie Moonlight."

"Trevante Rhodes." I licked my lips and nodded; eyes fixed on the photo we took together in his car recently. "Honestly? That's why he got my number."

Esme giggled.

I had yet to bring Nico around my girlfriends to meet them. I was still vetting and enjoying him all to myself.

"He is so sweet, Esme," I gushed. "He's a career man. Constantly working, which we'll have to change once we're serious. Most of our phone calls happen when he has to run to the supermarket or when he's in his car on his way home from work, but he always makes time to call and speak with me every day which is a huge plus to me."

"Oh, of course." She nodded. "What's his friends and family like?"

"I don't know." I shrugged. "I guess he's vetting me the same way I'm vetting him because I haven't met his family or friends yet either."

"Hmm." Esme shrugged too. "I guess when the time is right."

"Look at his smile, though." I blushed, taking one of my perfectly rolled locs into the pinch of my two fingers. I toyed with the loc as I stared longingly at our picture on my phone. "I swear he only smiles at me." I giggled. "All of his photos on his social page are of him mean mugging. But in the photo with us, all I see are teeth."

Esme laughed. "You got him whipped, girl."

"Sis, I'm as whipped, if not more."

"Do you want for me to whoop his ass?" Esme growled, shooting a look his way before returning her focus to me. "Because you know I will go over there—"

"No." I shook my head, eyes still on him... and the woman he stood beside. "Don't."

Nico towered over a table with a cake, surrounded by presents.

He smiled beside a very pregnant woman. I tried to not jump to conclusions, but there was no excuse I could make for the kiss he planted on her lips, followed by several more kisses to her cheek as the people closest to them snapped photos with their phones.

He wrapped his arm tight around the woman's shoulders, palmed her belly lovingly and smiled some more.

And my stomach muscles knotted.

Not because of the large blue and gold *Daddy to Be* pin he wore pinned to his white dress shirt. They knotted because of the position of his hand on her belly that gave me the perfect view of the white gold wedding band on his ring finger I'd never seen there before that day.

Don't you just hate it when married men cosplay as single?

I wasn't supposed to be *here*... at their baby shower.

Esme and I were on our way to dinner when she told me a teacher at the school Esme worked at was having a baby shower. Esme promised we'd only stop by the party hall for a little to drop off the present to her co-worker. We were supposed to stay for only a few minutes before heading out for dinner.

Never in a million years did I imagine walking into my boyfriend's baby shower.

"I need to get out of here," I announced.

"We'll both leave."

"No." I shook my head. "It's okay. You stay. She's your friend. I'm going home. I'm not even hungry anymore—"

"*You're* my friend." Esme took my hand and squeezed it. "And I'm not letting you go home alone like this."

I swallowed back my tears.

"To be real with you, Clarke, I barely talk to that woman. The only reason I agreed to come here was to see the baby's father. No one at school has met him before or after she got pregnant since she only started working there last September. I came here to be nosy."

"And I came to get my heart broken. Clearly." I scoffed a laugh. "This city is too small."

She shook her head. "I know."

"He's fucking married," I expressed low. "*Wow.*"

I looked away from Esme out of frustration and somehow locked eyes with Nico from across the party hall. He'd looked away from his wife for only a moment to see me still standing at the entrance.

His jaw dropped next. And like a pest scrambling when the lights get turned on, he whispered something into his pregnant wife's ear before stepping away to make his way over to me.

"I'm out," I decided, turning to leave.

I didn't even wait for Esme to respond before I was taking large steps out of the door.

Summer heat and honking horns from passing vehicles were there to welcome me back.

It was after six in the evening, the sun still out. Though the heat had reduced since high noon, it was still sweltering, making me feel more miserable than I already was.

"Clarke," Nico hollered at me from up the block.

I stopped walking and twisted around to find him jogging up to me.

"Clarke, baby," he said from feet away. "I can explain—"

The slap I gave him across his lying ass face when he was close cut his words short. Nico's hand flew to his cheek, and he took a step back.

I pointed at him. "That was for your pregnant wife and for fucking *me* when you have a pregnant wife."

"Clarke!" Esme shouted from up the block.

"You have a *wife*... and she's pregnant." I scoffed. "Congratulations."

"Clarke..." He held his hands out in front of himself. "It's complicated."

"I'm sure it's *not*." I flicked his pin with my finger. "Daddy to be."

"Nico!"

When I looked up the block toward the voice, I saw the pregnant woman who I presumed was his wife, holding her belly while staring at Nico and me with wrinkled brows.

"What's going on over there?!" She yelled next.

In that short time, a few people emerged from the party hall behind her, gathering on the city block just in time to take part in my humiliation.

I refocused on Nico and shook my head slowly.

"Clarke," Esme whispered to me when close. She glanced up the block at the crowd growing outside of the hall's doors, then at Nico, before taking me by my arm. "Come on."

Nico uttered nothing else, and it was probably for the best. Because there was nothing he could say to take back the feeling coursing through my veins.

I thought he was the one. *My* one. The guy God rewarded me with after experiencing the worst of the worst in relationships. Liars, narcissists, undercover man children. I'd had them all. I truly believed when Nico and I met that I'd arrived in the land of milk and honey. Nico was my trophy for not giving up on finding love in a city that constantly showed me none.

But he wasn't. And that fact was *so* damn sad.

So, I let Esme pull me away when she tugged on my arm a second time because my heart couldn't bear to take what my eyes let me see.

That I'd fallen for another emotionally unavailable man, an infidel this time, and again, I never saw it coming.

"You know what I was thinking about? No one ever talks about mourning the death of failed relationships they believed in." I lifted my white ceramic mug of black coffee to my lips to sip. "They always talk about what caused the breakup. The actual action that made one person say enough is enough. We hear all about the feelings in reaction to the breakup happening. But we don't talk about the death of the vision we all create when we are dating someone who we think we'll go the distance with.

We don't talk about all the time we spend imagining insignificant things like what it will look like wearing matching outfits. Or what we'll wear on our wedding day. What our children will look like. How we'll look together when we're old and gray... which you actually got to experience." I winked. "But for us mere mortals who don't get the forever we promised ourselves, that time and vision die a fiery, tragic death in a breakup. And we never talk about that. And we should because it's definitely a part of every failed relationship's life cycle, you know? That's why it takes longer than the time spent in the relationship to get over them."

"Definitely," my nana, Missy, concurred. She nodded slowly, lifting her mug to sip too. "So then, talk about it."

It was the next day after my Nico-is-married discovery and I was in my favorite place in the world - my grandmother's Park Avenue triplex.

She'd been living here for all 33-years of my life, and it has always been like my piece of heaven in a city that often felt like hell.

On a sunny Sunday afternoon in New York City, behind her big red door, I took a load off in a leather armchair by my nana's bedside. Like always.

She'd fallen ill shortly after my grandfather's passing five years ago. A severe stroke that forced her to learn how to walk, talk, and use her left hand all over again at 82-years-old. But nana did it with drive and grace. And at 87, although frailer than I remembered, and not well enough to be off her bed for too long, she was still kicking.

"What's on your heart, Clarke?"

This was our routine. My whole family's routine, actually. Spend time with my grandmother so she's never ever home alone. She had two in-home nurses, neither of them living on any of the three floors of Nana's triplex.

Her choice.

A morning nurse and a night nurse cared for Nana every day. But that left Nana alone in the afternoons and evenings. So, during those unattended hours, either myself, my mother, my father, or my older brother, Clyde, would fill in to keep Nana company until her night nurse arrived. My parents split Monday through Saturday, and my older brother Clyde and I took Sunday.

"I just feel so... sad and disappointed," I admitted. I rested my forehead into her warm open hand and closed my eyes, wanting to hideout in her touch. "But honestly... sad and disappointed doesn't even describe how I'm feeling. I'm more so..." I stared out of her glass window in search of the right word.

"Discouraged," she suggested.

"Yes," I exhaled with relief, closing my eyes to hold the tears in behind them. "*That's* it."

Nana may have been 87-years-old, but she was sharp as a tack and the only person I felt I could speak with and it feel like I was talking to myself.

My first name is her maiden name. She's my father's mother and one of my favorite people in this world.

"I just..." I straightened my back in the leather armchair to look into her eyes. "I can't believe this happened to me. *Me!* Of all people."

She knitted her brows.

I pressed my hand to my chest. "I *love* black love. I champion it. I have excellent representation of it all around me. Have had it all my life. Mom and dad. You and grandad. Monogamy is my jam and in the blink of an eye, *I* became black love's arch nemesis. I became the dreaded side-bitch."

"You didn't *choose* to be the side-bitch."

I scoffed. "The way his wife looked at me from up the block of where they were hosting their baby shower no less sure made me feel like the side-bitch. A home wrecking ass side-bitch."

I could never cuss this much in front of my parents. Even at my big 33, but Nana never gave a shit.

"You know what really bugs me, though?"

"What?"

"That I miss him." I hiked my lip up, sincerely disgusted with that. "I miss his lying, cheating ass."

She shrugged a frail shoulder. "You two just called it quits yesterday."

"*I* called it quits," I corrected. "*He* continues to insist he has a *complicated relationship* with his wife. He claims that before we started dating, he and his wife agreed to a separation. But we've only been dating for two months, Nana, and the woman looked two months away from giving birth. He's just so... *ugh*! Still lying. Still believes I'm dumb enough to believe it. I feel so stupid."

"Here you go, Nana," my brother, Clyde, announced from her doorway.

While I kept Nana company during our Sunday visits, big brother handled the cooking.

Clyde is a Master Chef at a restaurant in Brooklyn that earned a Michelin Star its first year in business. He has been knowing his way around a kitchen from the time we were kids. Two years older than me, Clyde behaved like he was more like a decade older... except with carrying on a secret relationship with my childhood best friend, Danyelle. He was real immature about that.

"Thank you, baby." Nana smiled big. "You know I love your squash soup."

He chuckled bashfully. "I'll be back with the brioche, some water, and your medicine." He pointed at her. "Don't drink even a spoon of the soup before you take your medicine, okay?"

"It'll be hard, but I'll do my best."

I snickered to myself, grateful for the change in feeling.

Staying home in my apartment simply wasn't an option today. I needed out. The night before was rough enough after Esme accompanied me home. We skipped dinner all together. I wasn't in any mood to eat. Nico ruined my expectations for our future together and my appetite.

"And to think," I jumped back in once we were alone again, "I actually almost canceled my group trip next week."

"The one to Maui?"

I nodded. "Nico had been trying to talk me out of going for the past few weeks when I told him my plans to fly out. Made a *big* fuss over me going because it's for singles and I wasn't single since I *now* had him."

Last year, during one of my lonely nights with wine, I was scrolling through my social feed and happened on a sponsored post promoting a group trip for singles. The caption boasted past trips to exotic tropical islands being a success, and I needed something different from spending another summer at a local beach. So, I booked the trip using my credit card last summer, forgetting all about it until a month ago. Thank God I was able to purchase round trip plane tickets last month, too, snagging one of the few seats left on both flights.

"Not knowing he had a whole wife, he failed to disclose to you," Nana mumbled.

"Exactly! The nerve."

"Here you go," Clyde said again, reentering our grandmother's master bedroom. He held his hand out with my grandmother's medication, and she took it, tossing the two white pills to the back of her throat while reaching for the water to drink next.

Nana held the crystal glass with one pinky sticking up as if she were drinking something fancier than spring water out of it.

I smiled at her daintiness.

Mrs. Missy Virginia Ali was my idol. A retired sommelier with a wine knowledge and taste palette I've always fawned over, Nana's love of wine and her pursuit to taste them all were birthed from her mother's, mother's inheritance of a Napa Valley vineyard in California. While Nana's mother inherited the vineyard from her mother and passed it down to Nana, my dad wanted nothing to do with it when Nana was ready to hand it over to him a few years ago.

My father, Jamel Ali, a corporate lawyer, hated wine with a passion. He was more of a scotch man. *Gosh*, does he love his scotch? Although he has taken on the responsibility of managing the wine barrel business that Nana also inherited and owns, Nana was forced to sell the vineyard after she fell ill and could no longer travel back and forth from New York to Cali.

I wanted that vineyard. I still do.

I went to law school to follow in the footsteps of my parents, who were both lawyers, but now I regretted that decision.

Unlike my father, I *loved* wine. With a passion. Nana had taught me everything she knew about how to taste wine and to taste the subtle notes in wine variants from the time I was eighteen.

Yes, eighteen.

She claimed if eighteen-year-olds can drink wine in Italy, why couldn't an eighteen-year-old girl from Long Island?

With each day that goes past, the idea of taking my love of wine seriously and following in Nana's footsteps becoming a sommelier myself gets stronger and stronger.

It may also be because I keep failing the bar in New York City and I'm slowly losing my interest in being a lawyer because of it.

I simply don't love it the way my parents do. Never have. Even while I was studying in undergrad or law school. I stuck it out though because my doing so made them so proud.

I loved the wine, though.

But with the vineyard now a distant memory, because of my father's disdain for the business itself, I really should kick the feeling of wishing it were mine.

"Clyde," I said, looking up at my brother. "Can you drive me to the airport next Sunday for a 10:30 a.m. flight?

"Airport?" My brother folded his thick arms over his chest. "Where are *you* going?"

"Maui." I forced a smile. "Ten hours to Honolulu and then an extra forty-five minutes to the island of two volcanoes separated by a valley."

"Nice." He smiled. "But I can't."

"Why not?"

"Sunday mornings are prime time at the seafood market at the pier. I wanna make Nana that stewed fish she loves so much next Sunday."

"You can still make it to the pier on time," I insisted. "Just drop me at JFK two hours earlier."

"Then I'd have to get up earlier on a Sunday losing extra hours of sleep I'm already *not* getting with a new baby in the house."

"Hey, hey! You *owe* me, okay, buddy?" I pointed up at him. "You dated my best friend behind my back."

Nana snorted a laugh.

He pointed back at me. "And I married her and gave you two nieces and recently a baby nephew, who I have to damn near pry away from you every time you visit because you love him so much."

"And I do... but betrayal is betrayal."

He kissed his teeth. "You do this shit every time I say no to you about something."

"7 a.m." I told him. "You can pick me up at 7, which will give you enough time to make your way around the market to get and make this beautiful queen here a delicious, stewed fish she loves and adores, as always."

Clyde grunted as he turned on his sneakers to head out of the room. Although I'm sure he was leaving to get away from me, he was likely on his way to the kitchen to clean up.

"Love you!"

"Yeah, yeah," he mumbled, crossing the threshold.

"Now," Nana voiced, drawing my attention back to her, "when you go on this trip, I want for you to arrive there with an open heart."

I rolled my eyes.

"Oh, don't do that."

"Truth be told, Nana? At this point? The only reason I'm going to Maui is because I paid for it."

She snickered.

"Plus, I desperately need a break from the firm since it's feeling like I'm doing my work, and everybody else's work, these days. I need an escape. This getaway is on time."

I ran my fingers through my locs and slouched back in the armchair. "I have no high expectations about finding love soon. I want to want it, but I just don't right now. I'm realistic. It is slim pickings out here. These men are *not* like the men of your time."

"Child, please." She fanned a wrinkled hand in the air. "In my time, men were not only carrying on relationships with women while married, but they were also creating entire families and living in them like they were the only family they had! The wives only discovered their side families when they showed up at those men's funerals instead of finding out about them online like how y'all do today. None of what is happening is ever new, baby. But just like there were good men back then, your grandfather being one of them, may he rest..."

I smiled at her, just mentioning him.

"... there are good men now. A lot of times you find them when you're not even looking. When you're just living, so do me a favor, beautiful granddaughter of mine."

"What's that?"

"Just live." She smiled big. "Go to Maui and live your best life, but keep your heart open. Promise?"

"Promise." I took her hand. "And you promise me something."

"What?"

"You live too... like, *literally*." I pointed at her. "Do not die while I'm on vacation."

She laughed.

"You laugh, but I'm serious! Do not die while I am in Maui, *please*. I'll be really mad at you, Nana."

"Only you would say some silly shit like that." She chuckled. "Goodness."

I scratched the back of my head. "I ain't hear you promise me, though."

That got some more laughter out of her and that made me laugh, too.

two

YUSUF

"TOMORROW IS THE BIG DAY."

I folded the last of my swim trunks into a neat square and placed it on top of the others I folded the same way.

"Flight is in the morning and these…" I held up the folded stack of swim trunks. "… are the last of my things."

I walked the folded stack of trunks to my opened hard-shell suitcase.

Glanced behind me long enough to add, "You get to be where you said you wanted to be, and you always get what you want with me. Even now."

I sighed over my luggage, placing my hands flat atop the folded clothes to lean my weight into the garments I'd placed in there from earlier. I pushed everything as flat as I could into the opened suitcase so I could zip it closed next.

"According to your mama, I've put this trip off long enough." I clenched my jaw. "And according to the group, she's right."

"God grant me the serenity to accept the things I cannot change, courage to change the things I can, and the wisdom to know the difference, living one day at a time; enjoying..."

Our voices echoed around the bookstore's basement as we continued reciting the prayer to close out our meeting. A routine we did every Wednesday evening.

Ever since my older brother Maurice pointed out that members at AA meetings recited the same prayer at their meetings, I was always reminded of that when we said it. We were kind of like AA members, if you really consider it. Trying to kick the habit of being so damn sad.

"Okay," Rylee announced. "That's all for tonight. As always, thanks for your presence. I'll see you all next week, God willing."

I'd been attending The Hope Collective for a little over a year. Heard about it through an online forum when I was up late one night fighting insomnia and a heavy dose of grief.

"Yusuf," Rylee called when I was steps away from the exit. "Can I speak with you before you leave?"

I briefly dropped my head forward, lifting it when I turned to face her, shoving my hands into my denim pockets next.

This evening's meeting was harder than others. I'd been dreading this week from the start of the month because of what I'd have to do at the end. Expressed that to the group which they were supportive of, as usual. They were also straightforward, which I didn't like, not tonight at least.

Rylee gathered her braids with one hand to move off her shoulders as she made her way to me.

She started the group in the spring of last year with the help of her therapist, Liz Peters. Liz attended meetings at the first of every month, offering counseling and guidance. She also gave us monthly action steps to assist with getting acclimated to our new normals, as well as journaling prompts to help with coping with our losses.

Rylee lost her best friend, Lennox Walker, after he died from a brain aneurysm in 2020. Everyone knew him as one of the greatest basketball players the Bronx Ballers has ever seen, but to Rylee, he was also the father of her two children. After his death, she believed there were people just like her dealing with the loss of a spouse or partner with no one to talk to who could really understand how they were feeling. So, she organized The Hope Collective, a grief support group associated with and funded by the Lennox Walker Foundation for Brain Aneurysms.

Rylee smiled and said, "I wanted to check in with you before you left. You seemed closed off today after you brought up traveling this weekend."

"I felt attacked."

"What?" She pressed her hand to her chest. "Oh God. Yusuf. I... I'm—"

"No." I chuckled. "Not like that. In a good way. That I didn't quite enjoy."

She motioned for us to clear the doorway so others could exit.

We held our support group meetings in a Cobble Hill bookstore in Brooklyn. Tiny space but very homely. You couldn't help but to feel comfortable surrounded by books even in a room with no windows. But every week was a struggle for me to deal with the truths the group forced me to deal with.

"Is this about—"

"Yes," I cut in, not wanting to get back into it. An hour was enough talking about it.

She held a hand up. "You know, the purpose of the group is to provide emotional support. We've all been where you are. We've all lost spouses and partners to brain aneurysms."

"Yeah, well..." I shrugged. "I don't see anyone else being pushed to rid themselves of the only thing that makes them feel like they still have a part of the person they've lost."

"You said those were her wishes—"

"Rylee," I groaned, running my hand down my face slow. "Please don't make me be a jerk towards you. You're super sweet and have been great with effortlessly welcoming me into this group when I walked in here a goddamn mess a year ago. I just... I'm just done discussing this. I don't

want to do what I must do, but everyone is saying I should and I'm tired of hearing about it."

She placed a hand on my arm. "If it makes you feel better, you wouldn't be the first person to be a jerk towards me when I was only trying to help, so don't trip about it."

I snorted a laugh, and she smiled.

"When do you fly out?"

"Sunday."

"If you need to talk—"

"I'll be fine—"

"You can call Liz—"

"I am fine," I asserted, backing away.

"You're going to one of the most beautiful places on this planet," she reminded me before I turned to leave. "She chose a beautiful place—"

"Not a bright side for me, Rylee." I crossed the threshold and headed for the stairs. "See you in a few weeks."

I straightened my back after I shut the suitcase and peered over at my wife's urn.

Purple with gold trimming, two of her favorite colors. Every time I saw those two colors together, I thought of her and all the good times we had while she was on this earth.

"I got the itinerary for the trip." I shook my head as I took a seat at the foot of the bed to face the urn. "They have a list of activities that I don't think I'll take part in, although your mother is begging me to. She does not know I booked this trip with a group for traveling singles and I have no intention of telling her that. Wouldn't make a difference, anyway."

It was the only way I could book the trip at a good rate. It included the price of the rented condo and resort amenities like food and drinks at some but not all of the resort restaurants, although I doubted, I'd partake in that either. All I was responsible for was purchasing the plane tickets.

Rylee announced to the group last summer she'd started dating again. Expressed the difficulties in that and the patience of her new guy. I admired her courage because I sure didn't have it in me to do all that shit again. Meet someone new, get to know them, fall in love, then build a life, only for the shit to be snatched without me knowing it would happen. All that work, all that time, only memories now that do nothing to fill the hole in my heart.

"God." I ran my hand down my face again.

I miss love.

The feeling of coming home to it. Sleeping with it. Feeling it all over me whenever it was near.

The stability.

The security.

I missed my wife too much, and even too much couldn't describe the enormity of how much I missed her.

"I'm gonna rest up," I said to her urn. "Although I don't have to get up too early tomorrow, the flight will be long, and I doubt I'll get any sleep on the plane. I never did when we traveled."

I stood to my feet and approached it, running the side of my hand down the smooth body. "We're going to your favorite place in the world, baby."

I released a deep exhale, feeling the pinch of tears in my eyes, and spun away, heading to the bathroom to get ready for sleep.

three

CLARKE

"EXCUSE ME, SO SORRY," I apologized, moving through the plane aisle and attempting not to bump the people seated or to spill my coffee on them.

I'd stopped at a coffee kiosk before arriving at the gate. I was on time at the airport, getting my boarding pass from the counter and making my way through the TSA checkpoint with no issues.

But I had to get coffee from the only kiosk in the terminal near my gate which sopped up a lot of time.

So much time, I had to speed walk to my gate after they made the last call for passengers to board the flight before they closed the aircraft's door.

I arrived in my section and noticed no one there. Most of the seats on the flight had someone in it. It delighted me to see my row empty. Since most of the people seemed to be on the flight already, that meant I'd have the entire row to myself.

"Yes!" I whispered, smiling big.

I pushed my carryon in the overhead bin and shimmied into the row, plopping happily into the window seat. My favorite seat on a plane.

Was it my assigned seat? No.

When I booked the flight last month, there were no more window seats available. But with my row presently empty, who cared?

I wasted no time getting comfortable. Lowering the tray in front of the empty aisle seat to set my paper cup of coffee on. I wanted to get settled in my seat before takeoff. I slipped my feet out of my Nikes and then the socks I opted to wear to avoid having to put my bare feet on the airport's floor at the TSA checkpoint. Traded my sneakers for flip-flops, wiggling my white pedicured toes in them. Pulled out my blue cardigan sweater and draped the cashmere garment over my shoulders, sure I'd feel the chill of traveling more than 30,000 feet off solid ground and in the clouds for ten hours straight.

"*Uh...* pardon me?" the deep voice asked above me and to my left.

I immediately glanced that way and did the cliché double take. You know the one when you look the first time, but not to really see anything. More so in reaction to satisfy being spoken to. But then you are so taken completely off guard to the point you not only *want* to look again, but you *must* look again to truly take a gander at what your eyes are seeing.

In my case, it is milk chocolate, a clear complexion and lips that slide so effortlessly over white teeth. Attentive eyes that are both soft and wise like they know things about this world I haven't uncovered, although the wearer of those eyes doesn't look much older than me.

"I think you're in my seat," he said next. His attention moved to the overhead bin, removing the strap of his carryon off his shoulder, and hoisting the bag in the air to slide into the bin as well.

And I watched the whole time. Like a perverted creep. Watching the muscles in his thick arms flex as he used his 5'11" maybe six feet frame to reach above him to secure his bag in the bin.

"*Umm...*" My eyes fell to his broad chest in his blue tee before I shook my head to gather my bearings. "No one was here so I..."

"Helped yourself to my seat?" He peeked down at me to smirk, then refocused on the bin again to push his bag securely into it.

I scoffed, then smiled, looking away shyly.

"It's cool," he conceded. "You can stay put. I prefer the aisle seat, anyway." He pointed at my coffee on the tray. "But can you—"

"Of course." I picked up my cup of coffee immediately and flipped the tray back into its upright position. "I was just getting comfortable. Ten hours is a long time, you know?"

He took his seat and filled the space between us with the scent of expensive cologne warming on his skin. "The time flies by."

I turned to face him, my eyes falling on a perfectly trimmed mustache and goatee combo. "Are you a frequent flyer to the Aloha state?"

"Oh, yeah." He reclined the back of his shaved head against his seat's headrest. "Hawaii is my second home."

His tone had a heaviness to it when he said that which was different to me. Everyone gets so excited when discussing Hawaii, whether they've been there before or never. They all seemed to have a perception of Hawaii. A perception that was everything positive. But his tone was void of the usual enthusiasm I was used to.

"Are you sure you're cool with me sitting in your seat?" I asked.

He looked my way and a small smile pulled at his lips. "One hundred percent."

He had these deep dark brown eyes that appeared black under the plane's lights.

"Let me at least buy you an inflight drink." I winked. "Nothing says sorry for hijacking your seat like free liquor."

That small smile grew into a beautiful beam of sexiness. I had to take a breath to behold to avoid swooning or melting into my damn seat.

"Be careful saying words like *hijack* on here."

I blew air through my lips. "Noted. But that smile you've got there might be just a little more dangerous than my words."

Couldn't help but to say it.

He chuckled and ran his hand down his lips.

"You're very forward," he acknowledged next.

"I'm very honest."

"Hmph," he huffed and nodded.

I liked his disposition. I liked it a lot. He wasn't easy to read, but he wasn't difficult to figure out either. Very cool, extremely reserved. I couldn't tell if he found me as intriguing as I found him, and I wouldn't let my ego force me to wait to find out.

"I'm Clarke," I offered. "And you are...?"

He rolled the back of his head on his headrest to look my way. He examined me for a moment, exhaled deeply next, then pressed his left hand flat against his chest and told me, "Yusuf."

My eyes moved to his ring finger and my smile gradually fell off my lips.

The tan line was faint on his left ring finger. But it was visible. A thin line that orbited the space beneath his knuckle. Enough evidence he wore jewelry there. Jewelry that has consistently taken up space on his ring finger long enough for the sliver of skin beneath it to be hidden from the sun.

My lids collapsed closed, and I kissed my teeth, turning to sit forward in my seat.

"Nice to meet you," I stated as dryly as possible.

Damn.

"Don't tell me you hate my name," he joked.

I loved his name.

But I didn't love the fact he was married. At least, I didn't love the fact his married ass was attractive to me. Not that it was his fault I found him attractive. It was just too soon after the shit that went down last week. My attraction to him triggered me. I couldn't hide how I came off because of it.

Instead of answering, I pulled out my earbuds and plugged the adapter's chord into my phone.

My assessment of him being reserved and hard to read went right out the door before they closed our plane door to prepare for takeoff.

It was easy for silence to settle between Yusuf and myself because of the video that began playing on the plane's screens displaying pre-flight safety briefings as the aircraft rolled down the runway.

The moment the video concluded, I plugged my ears with my earbuds, reclined back in my seat, and closed my eyes.

* * *

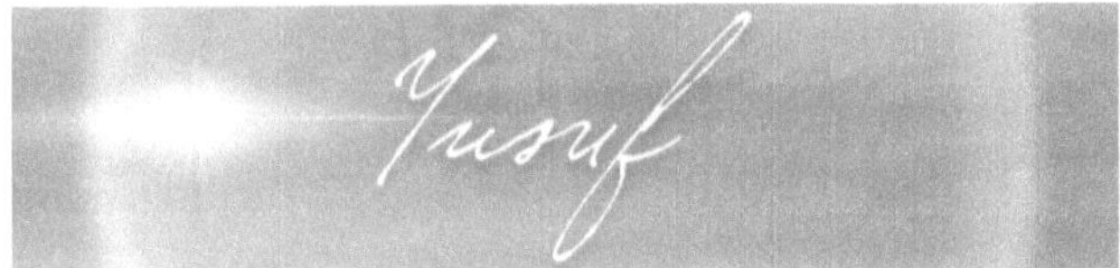

YUSUF

That was... weird.

Or was I weird?

Did I say something wrong?

Because what the fuck was that?

I had a lot of time to ponder all of that because of the long flight. And although in the past, time seemed to fly by, sitting in confusion sure made the hours drag for me.

We were officially six hours into the flight. I'd watched two inflight movies, played a game of Sudoku, accepted that free drink the woman next to me I now knew as Clarke bought for me, as promised, but I couldn't stay in the mystery of it all for too much longer.

I'd glanced at her to find her head resting on the lowered plane window cover. We were somewhere over California, and it was afternoon on this part of the earth. I should've been sleeping, but I always found it impossible to get any rest on the plane while crossing time zones even when my eyes were heavy.

I'd been glancing at her a lot since she practically shut down in front of me. Went from interested to dejected in the blink of an eye.

It was weird.

Or was I weird?

It's been a while since I've done this.

Flirt.

Or *try* to flirt?

I don't know.

Talking to women in that way didn't feel the same. I felt rusty. Like an old bike that's been in a shed for years and suddenly taken out for a spin without being oiled first.

The one taking me out for that spin was beautiful, though.

So exquisite.

Even as she slept with only her side profile in view in the aircraft's dim cabin only lit by the purple cove lighting.

She wore her long neat locs at the crown of her head in a messy bun. Now hidden behind closed lids, I remember how analytical her eyes were on me. Trying to search for something I wasn't sure she'd want to find. But I liked the attention. A little surprised by it. Before arriving at my seat, she wore a look on her face that many would identify as a resting bitch face. Didn't expect her to be so engaging. Actually, expected her to give me the energy she was giving me before she fell asleep.

All I told her was my name and she just... closed up.

And for the last few hours, I'd been trying to figure out what the fuck that was.

She yawned audibly to my right. I turned her way to find her stretching her arms above her head while sitting up in her seat.

Her bottle of water was to her mouth when I asked, "Had a good nap?"

The spout was still to her lips when she turned her head to look at me. She stared for a moment, leaving my question unanswered.

"Okay." I chuckled, turning completely to address her next with, "You gotta tell me what I said wrong."

"Excuse me?"

"Your mood," I continued. "It just switched on me like a light switch while we were conversing before takeoff, and I'm confused."

"*You're* confused." She scoffed.

"Very." I licked my lips. "Did I say something inappropriate? If I did—"

"You didn't," she confirmed. "And there's *nothing* to be confused about. I'm just... creating boundaries."

"Creating boundaries," I repeated.

"Yes," her eyes finally connected with mine. "Boundaries."

If she confused me before, she completely threw me now.

Was I *that* rusty? What did she even mean?

"I don't know where any of this is coming from but—"

"Do you *know where* your *wife* is?"

That hit me right in the chest.

She gestured at my left hand. "You're married, right?"

Yes.

No.

Shit...

My mouth hinged opened for a second before I gained the strength to lift and close it.

"Yeah, exactly." She shot me the nastiest glare a woman has ever given me. Ice cold and layered in judgement.

And I felt... guilty.

Not about her question, but because for the first time in a long time, I'd finally stopped thinking about my wife and that she was gone.

"The ring is conveniently missing, but the tan line is there and thankfully I noticed it." She shook her head. "Not about to catch me slippin' again. Because I was falling too damn hard and way too fast. Like always. Like an idiot. I clearly never learn..."

She kept rambling and my mind kept racing.

"You should be ashamed of yourself," she chastised. "Removing your damn wedding ring."

That brought me back into her frame.

"Or maybe I should be," she sniped. "You weren't really flirting, but you didn't give off the taken energy a married man should give off."

"I..."

... couldn't find the words.

"Why do you guys do this?!" she growled. "If you're unhappy in your marriage, just fucking leave, God! I can't even go on vacation and escape the nonsense. I must have a foul stench on me or something that attracts infidels. I may need a spiritual bath or something."

I cleared my throat and stood to my feet and left our row abruptly. Took large steps up the aisle and made my way to the far end of the aircraft to the bathroom. Someone occupied the bathroom closest to our row and, honestly, I needed space between us. The tiny twenty-four-inch-wide box of space the aircraft's lavatory offered wasn't exactly the space I needed, but shit, I needed away from *that*.

Did I know where my wife was?

Yes.

In my carryon in the bin over both of our heads. Reduced to ashes in an urn and on the way to the island, we both told each other 'I love you' for the first time.

And yet, there I was trying to flirt with another woman with my wife in a bin over our heads.

I swayed with the movement of the aircraft and peered up, staring into the lavatory mirror. Locked eyes with my reflection and had to look away just as fast.

Because she's right. I should be ashamed of myself.

four

CLARKE

ONE TEN-HOUR FLIGHT and then another short forty-five minute one on a smaller aircraft and I'd finally arrived in paradise.

I lowered my dark designer shades down the bridge of my nose to afford myself an unfiltered view of all the green and blue around me.

The weather was perfect in Kā'anapali, West Maui. The breeze was an excellent complement to clear, blue sunny skies.

Pure goodness.

I could feel any stress I may have had, including the jet lag that was slowly creeping up on me during the shuttle ride to the resort, dissipating completely once the ocean breeze glided along my skin. It was like the air was brushing my troubles off my shoulders like dust.

"Welcome to West Maui," the bellhop greeted as I crossed the glossy stoned floor.

He looked like a native of the island. Fair taupe skin with inky black hair. Around his neck he wore a floral lei with petals that blew in the tropical breeze rolling through the resort's entrance.

I smiled. "Thank you."

"Checking in?" He asked next.

"Yes." My eyes scanned around me. "I'm with HeartMates' Island Hop solo travelers group. I was told to give my name at the front desk, and you would give me my itinerary along with other things needed for my stay."

"Yes, of course." He gestured for me to follow him, and I did.

"You'll take this elevator to the third floor to check in and the front desk will assist with everything else."

"Thank you."

For my two-week stay, I packed light. All my stuff fit into the carryon I brought with me on the plane. When I traveled, I often filled my suitcase with things I hardly if ever wore during my stay and I wanted this trip to be different. Less baggage in my life and in my arms was the vibe I was aiming for. I figured if I needed anything while here, I could buy it.

Here was West Maui at a tropical resort that doubled as a condominium village. The entire area, as far as my eyes could see was surrounded by beach and picture-perfect rental condos. I planned to stay in one of those condos. A one-bedroom ocean view condominium with a living room and bedroom that led to a large patio that overlooked the blue turquoise North Pacific Ocean. The sponsored post online displaying a view from one of those patios sold me a year ago and had me reaching for my credit card.

"Welcome to Kāʻanapali," the pretty concierge greeted. Her eyes had a slant on both ends and she wore a white and yellow plumeria flower tucked in her hair. "May I have your name?"

"Thank you and sure. Clarke Ali. I'm a part of HeartMates' Island Hop solo travelers' group, if that helps."

"Yes." She nodded. "I have you here. Let me get you set up. Would you like your bags sent up to your condo ahead of you?"

"That would be great, thank you."

I allowed my attention to drift off her as she continued to get my room details in order. I tuned into her polite interruptions of my surveying the resort grounds from where I stood.

This place was truly magical.

The air smelled of relief and the vibe was relaxation. Even the workers who passed around me seemed like they were on vacay.

I've always wanted to travel to Hawaii, but the ten-hour flight from New York was always a turnoff and so was the cost to visit. But I just had to sign up for this group trip last year. The dating scene had hit the lowest of the lows and after careful thought, I realized I hadn't left New York in years. Me seeing the ad for the group trip seemed to pop up on my feed on time, and it ended up being much more affordable booking as a group, albeit with strangers, than had I booked the trip alone.

Flowering trees shading the balcony close to the front desk perfumed the air. I couldn't believe how naturally beautiful Maui looked and smelled.

It was like a scratch and sniff sticker come to life.

I giggled as I returned my attention to the lady on the other side of the desk I stood.

The elevator I'd just ridden on dinged, and the doors opened next.

Then I saw *him*. Swaggering out of the elevator with a bag on his shoulder and pushing a rolling suitcase in front of him.

And I did a double take again.

Not for the same reason I did when I first saw him on our flight over here.

"No. Way." My voice echoed around us.

His brows shot up, and he briefly faltered in step when we locked eyes. He blinked himself out of brief shock though, effortlessly, maintaining an even expression on his face, taking steps in my direction.

I rolled my eyes and turned to face the woman in front of me.

After arriving in the Honolulu airport, I'd quickly exited the aircraft without uttering another word to him.

Yusuf.

Of course, I remembered his name.

After he stormed off in the middle of me, chastising him on the plane, he returned to his seat and was quiet for the rest of the flight. Plugged his ears with the headphones he received from the flight attendant and kept his eyes on the screen ahead of him watching a movie.

And it was for the best.

I really had nothing else to say to him and was happy he had no more words to exchange with me.

But now he was *here*.

And a part of me was... excited about that?

I turned to look his way because of that.

He forced a brief smile as he stood at a comfortable distance behind me.

"Tiny island, huh?" he asked low.

"*Too* damn tiny," I countered, turning to face forward again.

"I think you've gotten the wrong impression of me—"

"Nope." I twisted quick to face him again. "I think I'm right on the nose about you, mister tan line, sir."

He swallowed hard and nodded, looking away.

"You're all set," the lady announced, holding out a thick folder of papers. She placed a tiny envelope on top and told me, "These are your room keys. Your bag should already be up in your condo. Everything you need to know about your stay is in this folder, but if you have questions, please be sure to ring us up from your condo's phone."

I thanked her and quickly excused myself, doing well not to make eye contact with Yusuf again.

Because I couldn't help my excitement seeing him here. Even if I shouldn't have felt it.

I pushed the call button for the elevator and tossed a last glance in his direction to see him conversing with the lady on the other side of the counter.

He really had a certain cool grounded aura about him that was attractive... to me, at least.

What were the odds, though, that he was not only on the same island as me? But in the same resort? At the same time?

That was trippy, no?

Riding the elevator up to my condo was quick. The design of the resort's condos was similar to that of a hotel, but with a more homely feel. My condo was near the top floor. And the moment I opened the door, the tunes of a ukulele-rich Hawaiian song playing from the living room's flatscreen greeted me at the door.

Whoever cleaned the room left the patio doors opened so the ocean breeze I fell in love with down in the resort's lobby was there to pull me into my home for two weeks.

I held my bottom lip in a bite and smiled at all the blue and green I saw ahead of me. Tops of coconut trees swaying with the air. The white froth at the hem of the ocean's shoreline that kissed the sand and retreated like a shy lover.

The bottoms of my flip-flops swept against the shiny natural stone floors as I entered the condo. I left my bag on the kitchen's island and stopped to peek inside of the Island Hop labeled shopping bag. There was a t-shirt with the Island Hop logo, a water bottle bearing the solo travelers' group logo... and a box of condoms.

I arched a brow when I pulled the box out of the bag to give it a closer inspection.

"Magnums." An impressed expression pulled at my lips. *"That's ambitious."*

It was a singles solo travelers' group, so I guess they were just covering all the possibilities.

But...

"I doubt I'll be using these," I declared, dropping the box of condoms back in the bag, then heading straight for the patio.

I passed a mounted flatscreen, entertainment center, and wood and wicker furniture decorated in blue and coral throw pillows.

My flip-flops made no sound once I stepped onto the carpet in the living room. And once I arrived at the patio's threshold, crossing over to feel the sun beaming on my brown skin, I smiled so big my cheeks ached.

This was paradise for real.

My phone was in my hand a second later, tapping the name of the person who made me promise to FaceTime her the moment I arrived on this patio.

As the call went through, I switched the camera's view to match my point of view of the ocean.

She gasped and swooned the moment she answered. "Oh. My. God."

"Right?"

Juliette smiled so big, eyes moving all over my screen. She wore her big copper curls up in her usual big bun. She pulled herself away from a broad chest in a tee to sit up in bed.

"It's beautiful," she gushed.

"It's paradise!"

She giggled. "What time is it over there? It's so sunny."

"Around 3 p.m.," I answered, walking my way to one of the patio lounge chairs to take a seat. "What time is it there?"

"9 p.m." She grinned. "I'm in the future."

I snorted a laugh.

She glanced to her right and blushed.

"Oh!" I smirked. "Did I interrupt something?"

"No," she whispered. "Not yet at least. Luke and I were watching a movie."

"Oh, and now he's trying to get the movie to watch y'all."

"Exaaactly," Luke confirmed in the background. "See? Clarke gets it."

I giggled.

The two of them have been inseparable since getting together earlier in the year. Former school rivals turned boyfriend and girlfriend. They were extremely cute. That's the only reason I supported that union.

Luke wasn't as bad as I thought he was when we were all in college. At least *now* he wasn't as bad.

Plus... they gave me hope to get back into the dating scene when I did.

Unfortunate part of that hope went up in flames after I misused it and was an unintentional other woman.

"I'll be back," Juliette promised Luke as she climbed off the bed and stepped away. "So..."

I crossed my ankles in my chair.

"How are you feeling *today*?"

I rolled my eyes closed, dropping my head back.

Juliette closed her bathroom door and took a seat on what I presumed to be her toilet seat lid. My girl lived in the cutest cramped Brooklyn studio co-op you ever would see. She made it work for her, though. But the only way she could get privacy whenever she had company was to escape to the bathroom.

"I'm better... well..." I rolled my eyes. "I'm better *now*, at least."

She tilted her head to one side.

"There was a guy I met on the plane."

"Oh?!"

"But he's married."

"Oh."

"Yeah. And the guy didn't even have on his ring. I only knew he was married because of the tan line around his finger."

"Damn."

"It's like..." I lifted and dropped my arm. "I have a sidepiece stamp tattooed on my forehead or something."

She giggled and stopped, glancing up to her left. "Yes?"

"You coming back out here?"

Juliette couldn't fight her shy smile even if she tried and I couldn't help but to blush watching her blush.

"I'm busy."

"I'm trying to get *busy* too," Luke argued.

Her jaw dropped.

"Clarke is in paradise and I'm trying to create a little paradise out there on that bed."

"*Shhh*," she shushed, pressing the phone to her chest making me only see black.

"Clarke is good," he added in the background. "Clarke, are you good?"

I laughed. "I'm great."

"Fantastic."

Her phone's camera shook a little as it was moved.

She gasped. "Hey!"

His face was who I saw next as he held the phone. Dark brown skin and eyes. I could understand why Juliette would get lost in it all. "Juliette's gotta go now. Aight, Clarke?"

I rolled my eyes playfully. "Okay, fine."

"Say, bye," Luke instructed, turning the phone to Juliette, who was fighting back her smile while shaking her head. "Bye girl. Call me anytime—"

"But not tonight," Luke added before ending the call.

"He is such an asshole," I said to myself, laughing.

I navigated my way to my contacts to place another phone call.

"And already she's glowing," my grandmother commented the moment she answered.

My brother Clyde and I taught Nana how to use a smartphone so we could talk to her throughout the day. Took some teaching on how *not* to hold the phone, so all we saw were her nostrils. But now, she got it.

"Am I?" I challenged.

"*Mm-hmm*, and from the little I see, it looks beautiful."

I turned the camera's view once more to give Nana a look at the ocean views this time. "It's gorgeous."

"Whew!" she gushed. "I tell you; Hawaii will *always* be one of the most beautiful places I have ever seen in my life."

I flipped the camera's view back onto me. "I might have to agree."

"How was the flight?"

"Long... a little frustrating."

She wrinkled her brows. "Why frustrating?"

"There was this guy on the plane. I stole his seat."

She laughed. "Clarke, what?"

I snickered. "He was fine with it. He was *fine*, period. Nana, that man has the energy to make me submit."

"Oooh, child, love him already!"

"But he's married."

"Oh, no, I don't." She made a face to illustrate her disapproval. "Leave him alone."

"And did, quick." I nodded. "The thing is, he's *here*."

"Where is here? In your condo?!"

"At the resort."

"With his wife?!"

"No." I shook my head. "Alone. He was alone on the flight, too."

"Traveling to Hawaii without his wife? That doesn't seem right."

"It isn't, now that I think about it." I twisted my lips to one side. "What's worse is he didn't have on his wedding ring. I only knew he was married because of the tan line around his finger."

"Christ." She shook her head.

I shook mine too. "Finding attractive men has never been an issue for me. Finding men who are loyal and have a proven track record of maintaining loyalty is where I always fall short."

"Give yourself grace, Clarke."

"Nana, I'm only being realistic. I know the only thing I'm going to find on this trip is myself, and that's fine. Men are a disappointment and an embarrassment, anyway. They're all liars. They need lies like they need air."

"Not *all* of them."

"*Most* of them."

"Well, put that out of your mind," she advised. "Because if you only focus on the bad, that is what you'll get. For now, just enjoy your trip, baby."

"And you don't die while I'm enjoying my trip."

She cackled. "You shush."

"I'm serious."

"And I'm going to bed, child."

"Fine. You just make sure you get up in the morning."

She laughed some more. "Bye Clarke. And remember..."

"Yes?"

She held up a wrinkled finger. "Have fun!"

* * *

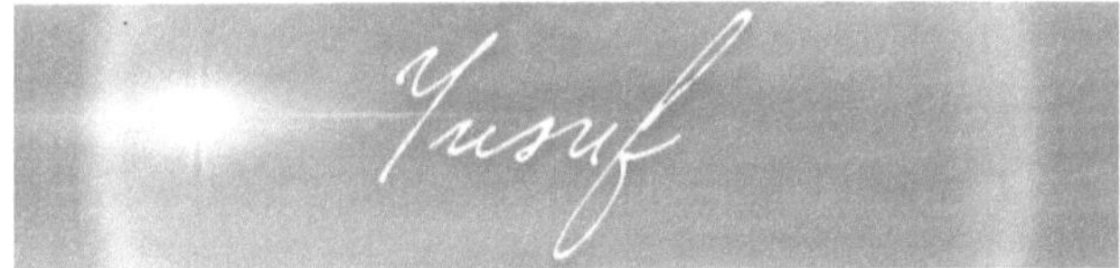

YUSUF

"And here we are," I announced.

I pulled my wife's purple and gold urn out of my carryon and placed it on the center console's marble surface. Stepped back and focused my view on the surrounding space.

I've stayed at this resort and made a temporary home in this condominium village plenty of times. Made many memories here that I'd been trying to suppress since arriving. To say the feeling running through me was bittersweet would be for lack of a better word.

I was both happy and very sad to be back. At least like this.

"As much as I want to feel like crap about all this," I said to the air. "Being here kinda makes that difficult."

I glanced to my left and half smiled at the mountain view.

This was always a topic of dispute for my wife, Parris, and I… where we would stay whenever we booked a stay at this resort.

She loved the ocean view for sunrises, and I loved the mountain view for the sunsets. We often had to play rock, paper, scissors to decide on what view we'd get whenever we visited.

The many times we've visited.

Together.

I blew raspberries with my lips.

This would likely be my last time visiting this island. I wouldn't be able to come back here after this visit. Not after keeping my last promise to my wife.

Coral pink and sea green surrounded me. Printed on throw pillows and in the paintings around the room captured swaying palm trees, and coral and starfish underwater.

The vibe in Hawaii was always one unmatched. There was simply nothing like it. I loved this island with everything in me. So much so, I felt myself beginning to miss being here, and I'd only just arrived.

"It's still a week, before your birthday," I said to her urn. "I'll have to find some things to do out here before then, which won't be a problem. Also, the plan."

I took a seat at the foot of the king-sized bed to face her urn.

I've been talking to her purple and gold urn since my wife's cremation and after they placed her inside of it two weeks after her passing. Talking to her urn made me feel like I was talking to *her*, and she was sincerely one of my favorite people to talk to.

She got me. Understood me. Sometimes I wouldn't have to say a thing and she would know what I was thinking. Her mother would often say we shared a mind. And I believed it.

I ran my hand down my close shaved head, then over my trimmed mustache and goatee.

"Although I've got an itinerary here, that will help keep my mind off everything. So far, everything here reminds me of you... including this woman I met on the plane on the way here."

I scoffed a laugh.

"She's intense, a little of a spitfire, and hard to forget, like you." I licked my lips. "She was hitting on me, much like you did when we first met. But she thinks I'm married. And I am. In my heart, at least I still am."

I stared at my wife's urn for a couple of breaths, saying nothing.

"You have nothing to worry about, though, Parris." I blinked back tears. "She's like you, but she ain't you. No one will *ever* be just like you, baby."

I swallowed hard, squeezing my lids shut and turning my head away.

"Nah." I focused on the mountains in the distance. "I doubt love will ever find me like that again. People rarely win the lottery twice, right? And I hit the jackpot with you."

I stood from my seat and took steps toward the patio. I needed the air.

"I love you, baby," I avowed, before stepping out onto the patio. "But I *hate* that you sent me here to do this."

five

CLARKE

"GOOD MORNING SOLO TRAVELERS! And welcome to day one."

Amongst a group of fourteen people, I relaxed at a table beneath a giant blue umbrella under the forgiving Hawaiian sun, attention homed in on the peppy thin black girl with long box braids.

"I'm Patrice, your group trip organizer and your point of contact during your stay here in Maui. Aloha!"

Though it was day one of our group trip, it was day two and a half for me in Maui. On the day I arrived, I spent most of my time talking to my grandmother then watching a little Netflix before I knocked out. On day one, the day after flying in, I could not move. I was beat. I spent the entire day in bed, completely jet lagged. My circadian rhythm was so off, moving from Eastern Standard Time to

Hawaiian Standard Time. I was in Maui, but my body felt like it was still in Manhattan. I was wide awake by two in the morning. I could barely make it out of bed this morning to attend orientation.

"You are here for thirteen days, and each day there will be one group activity planned for you to mingle and explore this beautiful island." She smiled big. "If this is your first trip with us, let me catch you up to what we at Island Hop are all about. Island Hop is a travel group sponsored by the compatibility app, HeartMates, which we encourage you to download while here in Maui. In the folder you should've received on arrival to the resort, you will find a special code you can enter to join this year's group filter that will pair you up specifically with members currently on this group trip, based on compatibility of course."

That was one of my reasons for signing up the year prior when I saw the sponsored post online. Dating was getting on my nerves, and I wanted to travel. What Island Hop promised, traveling with like-minded people, seemed right up my alley. I figured if the dating sucked while here, at least I'd have a beautiful island to stay on.

"We, at Island Hop, host solo vacations on islands *every* summer specifically for singles, and this year we are so excited to be on the small island of Maui. Our travel group is all about small groups, which we've divided into two groups of sixteen. The group we have assigned you to, my group, has members you have a lot in common with, so this should be fun. Here in Maui, we have a list of activities we will take part in that will range from sightseeing and underwater excursions that will allow you and your fellow solo travelers to make memories individually, but most excitedly, together. This is a singles solo travel group after all, so we encourage getting to know your fellow solo travelers..." She nodded exaggeratively. "And I promise you, you're in the perfect place to let your hair down and let your social flag fly!"

I glanced around myself, eyes landing on the fourteen faces I could see from my seat. Everyone was beautiful. Not beautiful from the lens of typical beauty standards, but definitely easy on the eyes.

Then again, in a place like Hawaii where feeling good and having fun is standard, being happy comes easy and happy is attractive in any form.

I recounted the heads, including mine, once again, quickly realizing the number was off.

She said sixteen, and we were only fifteen.

"Today, our activity is light," Patrice continued. "We're going to explore the grounds of the resort. There's so much to do here, so much to get into when you aren't hanging out with us as a group, and we want you to know *all* about what and where you can do those things."

I was gathering my locs to the top of my head to secure in a band when my perusing landed my attention on Yusuf.

Instead of securing my locs, I let them fall again, a little shocked to see him where I was once again.

It wasn't enough that we flew out here with each other and that he was staying at the same resort as me. But now I'd have to see him while I was out of my rental condo?!

What's crazier is the fact he was making his way to where my solo travelers' group gathered.

His presence intrigued me, though. Obviously, I was still stuck on the question of what he was doing here. But also... seeing him again was intriguing enough.

He wore casual clothing, but nothing on him looked inexpensive. From the shades over his eyes, the salmon-hued thin tee he wore over his broad chest with sleeves that hugged his thick arms. Linen cloud white shorts, or, as my girl Juliette called them, hoochie daddy shorts. Toned thighs that led to strong calves and nice toes in designer logo flip-flops. I could see the logo because he sure enough walked exactly where the group was meeting, stopping at the far end of where I unwound.

"What is he doing here?" I mumbled to myself. "I know he's not in *this* group."

"Okay, that's it!" Patrice announced, motioning toward one of the nearby buildings. "The first place we're headed to are the pools. There are several and spread throughout the resort and this resort is huge! But we'll start with the largest one. It's an infinity pool, too, guys. And it has a bar!"

I grabbed my tiny taupe crossover, slipping it over my shoulder and stood to my feet, directing my attention down to fix my yellow chiffon maxi dress.

I looked up in time to see Yusuf walking in tow with the rest of the members of the group.

"What are you doing?"

He glanced behind himself toward my voice and looked again, removing his shades to get a better view of me, I guess. "Oh, hey."

"Oh, hey?!" I questioned. "What are you doing here?"

"The same reason *you're* here?"

"That's interesting." People walked around us as he stopped to entertain my query. "This is a solo traveler's group... for *singles*."

"I know."

"Wow." I blinked a few times. "There is just no limit to your shit, huh?"

I turned on my jeweled slippers and stomped my way like a brat over to Patrice, who was leading the pack up ahead.

"*Umm...* Patrice?"

She stopped and turned immediately.

"Hi." I smiled, and she returned one back. "Can you assign me to a different group?"

Her thin brows shot up. "Why? Is there a problem?"

"Not a big one." I glanced behind me to see Yusuf swaggering past us. I followed him with my eyes before refocusing on Patrice. "I just think another group would best suit my interest."

She made a face one that clued me in on the response she gave me next, which was, "I'm so sorry but our groups are evenly divided into two and because our groups are small, we can't have one member more than planned. I can check to see if anyone in our other group wouldn't mind switching with you, but you'd have to give me time, a few hours, maybe, to ask around?"

"That's fine, I can wait." I nodded. "So long as it's possible and can be done, I'm willing to wait."

"No problem! Okay, so what's your name and room number?"

I gave all of my information to Patrice and rejoined the group, hoping I wouldn't have to wait too long.

We'd visited the infinity pool and were walking toward another outdoor pool when Yusuf caught up to me on our walk.

"Clarke, right?"

I sneered at him from the side of my eye, refusing to give him more attention than that.

"To answer your question," he started, "my wife is in a place I wish she wasn't."

That got my full attention and influenced me looking his way. "Excuse me?"

He removed his sunglasses again, this time sticking one arm of the shades into the top of his shirt. "The other day you asked me do I know where my wife was."

I blinked in response.

"*That's* where she is."

"In a place you wish she wasn't? What does that even mean?" I scoffed. "Did she leave you?"

"Yes."

"Well, good for her," I sniped. "I don't blame her."

"She died."

I stopped walking and so did he.

"My wife passed last year in March. In surgery," he revealed, looking me right in my eyes. "It was a routine surgery related to a brain aneurysm she had the year prior. We knew the risks. I was against her having the surgery. We had one of our biggest fights in our relationship over my stance regarding her going through with it. She wanted it. She persisted. I conceded. Here we are."

"Oh my God."

Our group was way up ahead of us, but I didn't care. He didn't seem to either.

He inhaled a deep breath, dropped his head forward, then quickly lifted it again to stare off in the distance for only a moment.

"I...*umm*." He chuckled lightly. "I had been wearing my wedding ring until last month. I'm in therapy. My therapist felt removing the ring would assist in the grieving process since, as he says, I'm having attachment issues because of my atypical grief. I still carry it, though." He shoved his hand into his shorts pocket, pulling out the white gold wedding band before returning it to his pocket again. "And *maybe* I have a problem with letting her go. Rightfully so. But I wouldn't call it an issue..."

"I wouldn't call it that either," I added. "Shit. Yusuf... *I*... I'm *so* sorry—"

"It's okay," he interjected, holding up a hand. "It's cool. I didn't tell you all that for you to be *sorry*. I told you so you could be *comfortable* whenever you see me around."

"Yusuf—"

"I don't want your sympathy," he blurted over me. "I've had enough of it. Over a year's worth."

I nodded.

"You getting aggy with me was actually refreshing." He smiled. "Everyone I know has been so gentle with me, so it was nice to be treated like shit for a little." He pointed. "So don't switch up on me."

I balled my lips to fight back a smile.

"Maui is small. *Tiny*," he explained. "I signed up to join this group trip, not to meet anyone. I joined to take my mind off some things while I'm here by staying busy with an itinerary I didn't have to plan. I may or may not run with you guys while out here, but Maui is small, so I figured we're bound to run into each other again while visiting. I didn't want you to feel any kind of way when we see each other in passing, and I don't want you to feel any kind of way now after I've told you all of this. Okay?"

I wanted to hug him.

I heard what he said, but I could see what he didn't say. He was hurting badly, and I likely made things worse with my bullshit from the moment the man got on the plane to fly here.

I'm a monster.

So, I figured the least I could do was agree to whatever he wished.

I nodded again and agreed with an, "Okay."

He smiled, backing away. "I'll see you around."

And just like that, he left me standing in the same spot - stunned, saddened, and feeling shitty for being such a bitch to him.

"Hurt people really hurt people, huh, Clarke?" I mumbled to myself, slapping my forehead. "Dammit."

six

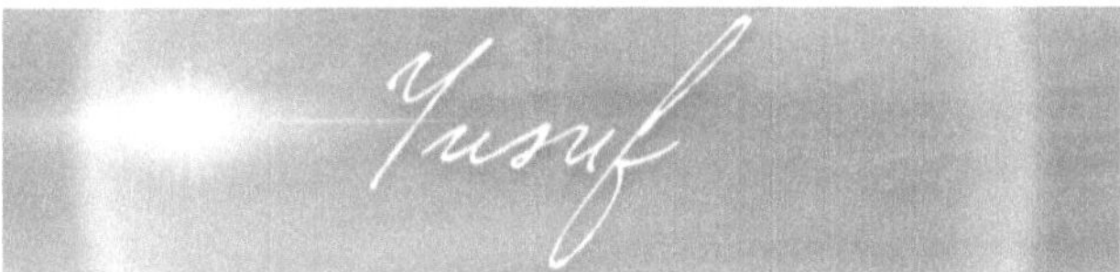

YUSUF

THE FINAL POPULAR amenity on the resort, a private beach with a manmade waterfall, was clear across the property and I'd had enough of walking. Parris and I, when we visited, would go to that beach near the leg of our stay at the resort because it was so far from our rental condo. Plus, by the time we were ready to head back home to New York, we'd run out of things to do and places to go. So, a long walk across the resort's grounds didn't seem unattractive.

It was to me this afternoon, though.

The group seemed over the tour after viewing the karaoke bar with the ocean view and I couldn't blame them. If this was the kind of activities this group's organizer had planned, I would have better fun staying in the condo most of the day.

But I'm biased because I've been here too many times and knew all the places. I had reason to be bored. Anything was better than feeling defeated, though.

"You know something we don't?" I heard behind me, pulling me from my thoughts.

Having spoken to Clarke more than enough times, I recognized her voice before turning to glance her way.

"Everyone's going that way..." She pointed behind us. "And you're going this way."

Clarke pulled her long locs to the top of her head and wore it as a bun. With her hair away from her face and off her shoulders, I could see the beauty in her features. Slender neck, petite shoulders. Her yellow summer dress molded to her slim but shapely physique like a seamstress sewed it only for Clarke.

"Everyone couldn't possibly be heading that way because *you're* heading here behind me."

"Yeah..." she conceded, catching up to me. "Because I'm trying to see if you know something we don't."

Her eyes were so beautiful. Intense. She held a stare that would challenge a meek man's ego.

I found it appealing. It made me curious. Posed the kind of challenge I liked because it kept me wondering if this would be the time she broke eye contact first.

I turned and pointed up ahead at the fleet of golf carts. "I'm renting the electric golf cart over there because between me and you, I'm done walking."

"*Whew*, same." She peeked down at her feet. "I did not wear the proper shoes for this."

That got a smile out of me. "Are you trying to help yourself to a seat on my golf cart the way you helped yourself to my seat on the plane?"

She gasped. "No! *Umm*... well... maybe?"

I laughed. "It's fine. Come on."

We approached one cart, and I waved my room key along the sensor to unlock it from its hub.

"How come I didn't know about these?"

"Because our group organizer hasn't told you all about it yet." I took my seat behind the wheel and Clarke took to the passenger seat beside me. Her perfume filled the space, and I inhaled deeply to hold on to the scent. "She's probably waiting to tell y'all when you get to the private beach. Probably knew you guys would want the cart and won't want to socialize on the way there. I'm thinking that's the plan."

"To play matchmaker?"

I peeked over at her. "*Mm-hmm.*"

Her attention lowered to my lips for a beat before she blinked her eyes away.

I started the cart up and steered the front wheels onto the paved road around the resort's lot.

The wind blowing along my face, driving in silence for a minute or two, with no thought besides going to the private beach, was a moment I wanted to stay in for a while longer.

Because when Clarke said, "Yusuf," I already knew what was coming next based on the careful tone in her voice.

"Don't do it."

"Do what?"

"What your voice is hinting you're about to do?" I glanced at her before focusing forward again.

The ocean was to our left, filling the air with salt and the scent of warm sand.

"I *have* to apologize."

"I don't *want* your apology."

"But—"

I brought the cart to a gradual stop, turned it off, and turned to look at her. "*What* did I tell you?"

"No sympathy."

"No sympathy," I repeated. "Then why do I feel I'm about to get more of something I'm already overfed on?"

She lifted her narrow hands and pressed them together. "I was wrong, and insensitive—"

"You were yourself."

"No." She shook her head. "Don't say that. I... *you* triggered me."

I knitted my brows over my eyes.

"My experiences with men have not been the best, okay?" she revealed. "I just broke up with one last week because he..." She stopped herself. "I don't want to tell my business like that..." Paused again and shook her head quickly. "Actually, no. I *will* tell it because I'm not *okay*. And I'm hurt and I'm pissed..."

I folded my arms over my chest.

"I found out my boyfriend, a guy who I *thought* I'd go the distance with, is married."

My brows shot up.

"And I found that out at his baby shower."

"*Shit.*"

"Right?!" she hollered. "Like what the actual fuck?"

"*Shh.*" I shushed while laughing. "You're pissed. I get it."

"I'm livid!" She corrected. "And mortified. And hurt. And a damn trashy 90s daytime talk show segment. *God.*"

"I'm sorry," I told her. The water gathering in her eyes made it impossible not to apologize.

"Well." She looked away. "If you say sorry, you're gonna have to accept my apology first because you did nothing to me, but I was terrible towards you."

I twisted my lips to one side and shook my head, starting the cart up again.

We were rolling along the smooth road of the resort, nearing the private beach up ahead.

"Did you enjoy being married?"

"Loved it," I answered.

"How long were you two married for?"

"Eleven years."

"Eleven years?!" She leaned forward to meet my eyes. "How old are you?"

"31."

"That's it?!" she shrieked.

I chuckled.

"You're young. And you're younger than me."

"How old are you?" I glanced to my right. "If you don't mind me asking."

"33."

I made a shrugging motion with the sides of my mouth. "You're not much older."

"Yeah, but... you're like... *way* more mature."

"Life does that to some people."

"Right," she agreed low. "Yeah."

We arrived at the entrance of the private beach and stepped out of the cart. Got there before everyone else expectedly.

"Wow," she exhaled. "I love this."

I could still hear Parris's voice in my ear standing there.

Clarke nudged me on the shoulder. "So, like, that means you and your wife got married when you were teenagers."

I smiled. "Yup, nineteen. Met in college freshman year. Married at City Hall by sophomore year, pissing off everyone around us." I laughed this time. "The only person who knew we did it was my older brother who was our witness."

"Why so young?"

I peeked down at her.

"I mean... it was obviously for the best, right? Because you two could get so many years."

"They weren't enough," I confided. "Eleven years weren't enough."

"No, I didn't mean—"

"It's cool," I interjected. "You're good."

We were quiet again for a few beats until I told her. "I was in love. *Very* in love."

She looked up at me to my right.

"I asked my wife to marry me because I was in love with her and didn't feel like waiting for what people kept telling me would be at the right time. *That* was the right time. Nineteen and eleven years wasn't enough."

"Oh!" we heard behind us. When I turned that way, I found our group's organizer, Patrice, inching closer to us, with the rest of our group close behind her. "You two got here fast."

"We rented a golf cart," I broadcasted, arching a brow.

"*Oooh*," she held up a finger and donned a teasing smile. "Sneaky, sneaky."

Clarke and I laughed.

"Clarke," Patrice spoke again. "I spoke with our other group organizer. He found someone to switch with you if you're still interested in changing groups."

I jerked my head back.

"That's okay." Clarke cleared her throat. "I'm okay here."

"Perfect!" Patrice commented. "Definitely happy to keep you here. Okay, everyone." She turned to address the group. "Here is the private beach! Can we just look at that waterfall?!"

I leaned in and asked, "Thought about changing groups, huh?"

Clarke opened her mouth and closed it. "I was... *really* triggered by your tan line."

I smiled, then shook my head.

I'd just stepped off the elevator and onto the floor for my condo when my phone buzzed in my pocket. After hanging out with the group and Clarke on the beach for a while longer, I left, leaving her behind. I returned the golf cart to the lot and walked the rest of the way to the condominium village on the resort.

"Yeah," I answered.

"Baby bro," my brother Maurice said on the other end of my phone. "How's it going?"

"It's going?"

I needed the time alone again. Though the plan was to spend as much time out of the condo and with complete strangers, leaving my mind less time to wander, I was ready for some solitude again. Likely for the rest of the day.

"How's Maui?"

I licked my lips, dipping my hand into my shorts to pull out my keycard to unlock the door of my condo. Inhaled a deep breath again when the door opened and I was treated to fresh air blowing through the open doors of my patio. The stunning view of big green mountains was an added bonus.

"Beautiful, as always," I answered, walking in, eyes fixed on the mountains. "How's New York?"

"Muggy, as summer always is here." He groaned. "Summer raining at night, and hot as hell. You know it's bad when it's eighty-nine degrees at 9 p.m. and the rain doesn't even help things cool down."

I chuckled lowly.

Since the view was so enticing from my front door, I headed out onto the patio and grabbed a seat in one of the lounge chairs.

"So, Maui's beautiful, I know that," he started. "But how are the ladies out there this time of year?"

"I wouldn't know." I brushed a hand down my mustache and goatee. "I haven't been looking."

Well, that wasn't all that true, right?

There was Clarke. A woman who, to me, was too damn beautiful not to look at. But her beauty came second to how she made me feel. Something I'm sure she didn't know she was making me feel... everything other than sad. More than that, she reminded me of what I remember life feeling like before the grief.

I wouldn't tell my brother Maurice that, though. Because then he'd have questions. Questions I'd have to use my memory to answer, which would entail me having to think of Clarke to recollect and I didn't want to think about Clarke when I should think about my wife.

"Besides, the single women, at least the ones in my age box, said they're fed up with our asses." I snickered, remembering my conversation with Clarke on our way to the private beach. "We've burned them too many times, so they have a wall up that I just don't have the energy to help tear down, you know?"

"Oh, I know." He laughed. "Man, I was single for a few months when Lena and I had that big fight and split up in 2015, and that was enough. I wanted back in a relationship with her real fast when I started dating again because the scene was bleak. It's a shame shit hasn't changed after all these years."

"Hmph."

My brother and his wife were the couple you couldn't imagine *not* being a couple. It's always been Maurice and Lena. A pair we all saw as one person. When they broke up, I remember my brother taking it really hard.

"Not having a wife is just not an experience I care to know anything about anymore— ooops! *Shit*. My bad. Damn. I didn't mean that—"

"It's fine," I jumped in. It felt good being able to have a genuine conversation with people again, especially family. For the past year, everyone has been so careful speaking with me, not wanting to say anything that might be a trigger that reminded me my wife is dead. But she was, and as time has shown, life continues to go on.

"I know what you mean," I added. "Not being married is not a thing I care to know about either."

"I didn't mean it like that—"

"Yeah, you did." I smiled. "And it's cool, I swear. It's okay. *I'll* be okay."

"Yes, you will," he concurred.

I nodded; eyes focused forward on the big, beautiful mountains. "'Cause I've got Maui, and at least thirteen gorgeous sunsets to bid farewell to for the last time. I doubt I'll be back here ever again after next Saturday."

"I'm proud of you, Yusuf."

I twisted my mouth to one side to bite inside my cheek. A habit to help keep the tears in.

"I know it isn't easy. I know a lot of the things you've *had* to do, what you've had to *agree* to aren't things you've *wanted* to do. But you're doing them." He huffed. "My baby brother is stronger than his big brother."

"Stop it."

"I swear to God, Yusuf," he insisted. "Got married before me. Lost your wife..." He sighed. "You're stronger, man."

"Well, what they say is true." I shrugged. "The raw deal in life is you never know your true strength until being strong is what you *must* be. When you have no other option, except to be strong."

He blew air into the phone, then said, "Absolutely, bro. That's real. And I'm here for you. Anytime. You know you can call me with anything, anytime, right?"

"I know."

After ending the call with Maurice, I remained out on the patio. Eyes fixed on the mountain view, fighting my thoughts and where my mind kept drifting them too.

Fighting them because I was getting what I wished for. To fill my time with things to distract me from feeling so sad.

The only thing was... that distraction arrived as another woman.

Clarke.

And I really didn't want that kind of distraction. Not while I was here. Especially when the *only* reason I was here was because of my wife.

seven

CLARKE

I SWITCHED my hips from left to right, draping my damp beach towel over my arm.

The sun was out.

The sun was always out in Maui. At least, in the three days I'd been there. And the weather was as consistent.

The temperature never got higher than eighty degrees. The breeze assisting with it feeling more like seventy-eight.

I absolutely loved it and knew it would be the one thing I'd miss the most once I flew back to New York.

I'd just returned from an activity with the Island Hop solo travelers group.

An outing Yusuf was visibly missing from.

Which disappointed me... a lot. Something I wouldn't admit to myself.

We visited Wai'ānapanapa State Park which was a remote, wild, volcanic coastline that was more like a beach than a park. I learned that many of their "parks" looked like beaches in Maui. The one we visited had calm waters and black sand created from volcanic lava, which intrigued me the moment we arrived. But while the park was interesting, my group was painfully boring.

Patrice was great, but there was so much she could do to keep the group exciting. If they were here to meet people, I couldn't tell. People barely spoke to each other.

I ended up leaving after half an hour of being there with them. There was a resort shuttle that left every thirty minutes from the black sand beach that I was lucky to catch back to the resort.

Back at the resort and on my way to my room in the condominium village, I spotted Yusuf sitting at one of the outdoor tables. In his hand was half a pineapple with the insides removed and filled with rainbow colored shaved ice.

"So, you chose shaved ice over our group activity?"

He peeked up and gave me a closed-mouth smile as he chewed. "And judging by how soon you've returned, I made the right choice."

I slid into the seat across from him, draping my towel on the back of the chair behind me. "They are so boring. My God."

He snorted a laugh, bringing his fist to his mouth to cover.

I giggled in response. "I'm serious. No one talks to each other. We're all there, following Patrice who, bless her heart, is doing her very best to keep us entertained. But sis sounds more like a travel agent than a group organizer."

"What were you expecting?"

"Honestly? Freaknik."

Both of his brows shot up. "I didn't take you for the type."

"Then don't judge this book by her cover."

He hollered a laugh this time and showcased the most beautiful natural white smile.

I bit my bottom lip, quickly identifying my favorite thing about Yusuf.

I had to get it together, though.

Down, girl.

"Okay." He nodded, getting out the last of his humor while placing his pineapple on the table in front of him. "Noted."

"I was *also* expecting *you* to be at the group activity."

He licked his lips. "And why were *you* expecting that?"

"Well..." I moved my locs off my right shoulder. "You *are* in the group, and we are all here to explore Maui *together*."

"Oh?" He pressed his shoulders to the back of his seat. "You mean the group you wanted out of because of me?"

I dropped my jaw exaggeratively. "I thought we got past that. And you won't let me apologize so..."

"I'm just messing with you." He told me. Yusuf picked up the tiny square napkin on the patio table to clean his mouth. "We're good."

"So then, if *we're good*, why'd you skip out on the activity today?"

"I knew I wouldn't miss much. I've been here plenty of times. There are certain things you do in a certain order to make the most out of your stay in Maui."

"If you've been here so many times, why'd you sign up with a solo travelers group to visit *this* time?"

He ran his hand down his mouth, and his goatee. "I needed an itinerary to fall back on, on the days I needed a distraction."

I tilted my head to one side, genuinely confused. "I don't understand."

He exhaled and smiled, looking off into the distance. "What are you looking to get into while you're here? What would make Maui what you envisioned?"

"Hmmm..." I turned my eyes up to the clear blue skies above us, thinking. "Fun. An experience I'll remember forever. Moments I can't capture on a camera. Anything, honestly, powerful enough to wash away the shit I got on me a week before flying out here." I shrugged. "I don't really know. I signed up for this trip last year.

When life had me bored out of my mind with the monotony of every day."

He nodded.

"I'm a paralegal." I scoffed a laugh. "And it is a job, not a career, and it is sucking the joy out of my life every day I show up for work. But I can't do anything about it because I keep failing the bar."

"The bar is hard."

"The bar is a pain in my ass." I dropped my back against my seat. "I don't think I want to practice law anymore either, but." I lifted, then dropped my shoulders. "I'm 33, almost in my mid-30s. I've finished four years of undergrad, two years of law school. I don't have kids, but I want them. I'm not even married, but I want to be. Life keeps life'ing and I have very little to show for the time that has passed. I've invested all this time. Time, I can't get back."

I locked eyes with him and sputtered a laugh. "And I don't know why I told you all that."

He smirked. "Maybe because you'll never see me again after this trip."

I pointed at him. "That's it."

Yusuf chuckled.

"So..." I dragged out. "I can't travel the world drinking wine on every continent, which would be my dream life. I signed up to hang out with a bunch of people who joined a singles group to remain single. Apparently."

"If you want adventure and you're not afraid to step out of your comfort zone," he started, "I know of a few places on the island you'd love to see that the group won't take you."

I perked up in my seat. "Yeah?"

He nodded slowly. "I mean..." He scratched his shaved head next. "I didn't really *plan* to go to these places, but I guess since I won't be back here again—"

"Be back where? Maui? Why not?"

"You ask a lot of questions, huh?"

"Hey!" I held a finger up. "I just told you something super

personal about a career choice I've told no one, including my closest friends. I can ask an intrusive question or three."

Yusuf twisted his mouth to one side.

Noticing his discomfort, I told him, "You don't have to tell me if you don't want to."

"Okay, cool." He nodded. "Thanks."

"Damn."

He laughed.

I laughed too. "I didn't mean that, you know?!"

"Do you want to go somewhere fun or not?"

A breeze passed between us, sending a chill down my spine. Wherever we were going, it would be only us two, no group of people showing up after or even later. Just us. And that excited me.

"Definitely," I replied.

"Okay, cool." He clapped his hands once and rubbed his palms together. "There's a catch."

I arched a brow.

"You can only say 'yes' when you hang with me."

I blinked hard. "Excuse me?"

"Comfort zones are fun's arch nemesis. The word 'no,' although it is a complete sentence, is also a gateway to limitation. There's no fun in limitations, Clarke."

I couldn't help the smile pulling at my lips. "Okay…"

"So…" Yusuf moved to the edge of his seat. "When you hang with me, 'yes' is all I wanna hear. Because 'yes' means adventure. And that's what you want, right, Clarke? Adventure in Maui?"

"*Mm-hmm.*" I nodded.

"All right."

I stared at him, and he stared back.

"I am both intrigued and concerned," I admitted.

"Perfect." Yusuf pushed his seat back, revealing the black basketball shorts he wore with his crisp white tee. "Then that means it's time for us to go. You'll need to change before we leave the resort."

I peeked down at my yellow bathing suit.

"You'll need sneakers for the hike."

"The hike?"

"The hike," he repeated.

"Should I be worried?

Yusuf shook his head next. "All I know is a good time. And I promise… you're safe with me."

* * *

What Yusuf failed to tell me was how *unlike* a hike it would be.

Unlike a hike in a great way.

I expected dirt path roads and steep hills. Dirt and dust being kicked up into the air as we trudged up mountains. I'd already decided when I returned to my rental condo, I'd have to wash my locs. I figured the black sand from earlier and the dirt from the hike would have to be washed out.

I was so wrong… about it all. And I'd never been so happy to be ignorant.

"Wow," I exhaled behind him.

He brought me to a rainforest.

A real-life rainforest. I'd only seen them in academic textbooks or on animal documentaries I watched while channel surfing. But pictures failed to compare to the real thing.

It was very green.

Literally, all I saw was various shades of green.

Long stalks of solid bamboo extended high above our heads, reaching for the sky like thin skyscrapers without windows, garnished by greener leaves.

The sounds of natural wildlife and water sloshing against smooth rocks in the distance were like a never-ending soundscape.

We used flat rocks to cross to the other side of the rainforest. Walking through a pond of clear water, I could see straight through. I caught glimpses of colorful fish in a pastel rainbow of colors swimming beneath our sneakers.

Yusuf and I caught one of the resort shuttles and rode the Road to Hana - a 64-mile-long road that extended to Northeast Maui. We rode on that road for a little over thirty minutes to visit a place, more like an oasis, known as Pua'a Ka'a State Wayside.

Yusuf and I passed a few groups of people on our trek through the bright green rainforest, sharing only pleasant greetings with them.

Before we left the resort for the shuttle, I arrived to him in the resort's lobby, dressed in a Brookville U tee, cut-off jeans and sneakers on my feet; my arms swinging, as instructed for me to do by Yusuf. I would've thought to bring my purse to hold my phone, but he insisted not to bother... with the purse. Not my phone.

My phone was in his backpack, a backpack he carried strapped to his back. With no phone screen to occupy my attention, I treated myself to a view I'd never forget.

We'd been walking for ten minutes when he turned to glance at me over his shoulder to inform, "We're close. Do you hear it?"

"Hear what? Besides all the other magical sounds, giving me an eargasm in this rainforest. Which pause for reaction... I'm in a goddamn rainforest!"

He laughed. "The waterfall."

"A waterfall? There's a waterfall here, too?"

"There are several."

He stopped at an entrance shaded by giant green leaves and pointed. "But *this* waterfall is the best one."

Like a painting that came to life is what it was. Or a painting in 4D.

To call the waterfall beautiful would be lazy.

Magical?

Close.

Majestic?

Yes.

Blue, white water seemed to fall from heaven as it cascaded

between two hills covered in vegetation. The body of water was too small to be a lake, but way too large to be a pond.

The sounds of water falling into more water was such a soothing sound. I could feel all my stress, any worries, all the negative emotions or feelings in me leaving through my pores the longer I stood at the entrance watching the earth show off.

"Yusuf." I turned to look at him.

He smiled big. "I know."

Yusuf gestured through the opening and said, "Let's go in."

I blinked hard. "Let's go in, where?"

He chuckled, stepping over the rocks that blocked the entrance.

"Yusuf," I stage whispered.

I watched him step through ankle high grass, removing his backpack along the way and dropping it beside his feet.

I folded my lips into my mouth and bit them closed when I wanted to protest. Inhaled an encouraging breath and stepped through the leaves and into the space close behind him.

I stopped beside him and said, "This is beautiful."

"Seeing it is one thing…" He pulled at the hem of his white tee, lifting the shirt up and over his head. "Feeling it? A whole unique experience."

My eyes rolled down from his and onto smooth, milky brown skin. Tiny sparse of coily hairs were scattered down the valley of his broad chest. Yusuf was solid, but not a muscle head. Slightly defined muscle covered his arms, chest, and abs, but there was nothing obnoxious about it. A thin line of hairs extended from beneath his navel, pointing the way to the v-line that disappeared into the band of his black basketball shorts.

My eyes lingered on the curve where his crotch was. "I brought nothing to swim in."

"Neither did I."

That got my attention and forced me to meet his eyes again. "Then…"

His hands were at the band of those basketball shorts before I could finish my sentence, using his grip to pull the shorts down and off.

My jaw dropped the moment those shorts fell to his ankles. My jaw continued to drop even farther. Because of my new view...

Yusuf's dick.

"Oh my God."

It was thick. So thick.

Like a bamboo shoot?

That was the first thing I noticed. The next thing I realized was he manscaped around that beautiful thick dick.

"Oh my God," I repeated.

Sex toy companies would pay dividends to use his dick as a mold for their dildos. I just knew it.

I couldn't take my eyes off it. Even as the thick muscle swayed between his thighs as he stepped out of his sneakers one at a time. I prayed I wasn't visibly salivating. Because in my head, I was choking on that thing.

He turned to face the waterfall and approached the pool of water feet away from the grass. I observed the rise and fall of his perfect ass as he walked his way to the edge of that water, balanced himself on the arches of his feet, and used his hind legs as momentum to dive into the water, headfirst.

His disrobing froze me in the spot he left me. He popped up through the water's surface, swiping water from his face with his palms.

He motioned at me. "Get in here."

"*Uhh...*"

"Don't tell me you're shy, Clarke." He bobbed up and down in the water and all I could imagine was what his dick looked like in the clear blue water.

Because it looked delicious on land.

"I'm... I'm *not* shy." I blinked repeatedly. "I'm shocked."

"Shocked?"

"I... I just saw your dick!"

He hollered a loud laugh.

I pressed a hand to my chest.

"What?" He bit his bottom lip and smiled menacingly with his fine ass. "Don't tell me you've never seen a dick before."

"I... have." I licked my lips and looked away to pinch the space between my eyes. "I've never seen the dick of a man I literally only met less than 72-hours ago."

"Clarke?"

I focused on him again.

"You're not about to punk out on me right now... are you?"

I rubbed my lips together.

"Or did I misunderstand the bored woman at the resort, who claimed she wanted an adventure?"

I pressed my tongue to the roof of my mouth and stopped myself.

"You wanted an experience you'd never forget, right?"

I bit inside my cheek.

"Everyone knows this park for their waterfalls and the waterfalls' healing properties. A waterfall shower is a *must* whenever you visit. This is the adventure you won't forget anytime soon *if* you step out of your comfort zone and get in."

"Oh, I'm sure." I laughed nervously. I turned to peek behind us next. "What if someone—"

"No one will come," he promised. "I've visited here more than enough times to vouch for this spot. It'll be our little secret."

I swallowed hard.

"You're safe with me, remember?" He reminded. "I don't take those words for granted, nor do I just say them because they sound good."

The decisive look in his eyes was serious. Sincere. His words were as solid as his form bobbing up and down in that water.

I exhaled the tension in my body, then used my right foot to assist with stepping out of my left sneaker then used my left foot to step out of my right. My hands were at my BU school tee next. I pushed air through my lips when I removed my shirt to reveal the brown bra I wore underneath and the matching panties when I took off my shorts next. And Yusuf watched me the whole time as I rid myself of my clothing.

All of them.

By the time I was taking steps toward the water, feeling my cheeks lift and fall with my movements, I was completely naked, not as subconscious as I thought I'd be once my feet felt the chill but warm presence of the water. And by the time I jumped in, submerging my entire body into the depths of the pool of water, I felt so free.

I popped back up, feeling for the floor of rocks and sediments beneath me with my toes. Pearls of water rolled down my locs, the cool air brushing against my wet skin. I used my hands to clear my face of the excess water. When my vision was clear enough, I noticed Yusuf was swimming toward the waterfall. So, I followed him.

The closer I got to the tiny waterfall, the more natural force I felt against my body in the water. The sensation was nothing I'd ever experienced before.

We were feet a part, standing only inches away from where the waterfall ended its cascade to become one with the water we stood in when I turned to him.

"You just saw me naked."

Yusuf focused on the waterfall when a grin appeared on his lips and he added, "Butt ass naked."

I pushed my tongue into my cheek to hold back my laugh.

"And I thought the waterfall would be the most stunning sight out here today." He turned his head in my direction and winked. "I was very wrong."

I smiled shyly next, rolling my eyes away to hide I was blushing.

"I'm thinking that was your reason for inviting me out here, Yusuf. To get me naked."

He licked his lips and lowered into the water, facing me. "You wanted adventure."

I smiled big, bending my legs at the knees to lower myself into the pool of water too. "This is definitely adventurous."

"And you have to admit." He smirked. "It was a good plan."

I gasped.

"You wanted Freaknik. I gave you Freaknik." He raised his arms out of the water to gesture around us. "The private Maui version."

I pushed water in his direction, splashing him and he returned the action, sending me into a giggling fit.

"Well... It's beautiful. Stunning," I told him when our humor settled. "Thank you."

He bowed his head, and gestured toward our clothes. "Ready to continue the hike?"

I nodded.

"Come on. I brought towels." He took off swimming.

"Towels?" I shouted behind him, my voice echoing around us. "So, this *was* your plan!"

All he did was laugh, and I couldn't be mad. Didn't have time to. Because all I could do was swoon when he walked out of the pool of water and onto the grass, giving me one last view of his perfect ass.

* * *

"Say what, now, Clarke?"

I giggled at Esme's reaction.

Night had fallen on the island of Maui. It was officially midnight, and I was wide awake and talking to my friend Esme on the phone.

Esme worked at a school in Harlem. She usually started her days at 4 a.m. and would often arrive at the school she worked at around 6 a.m. With school out for the summer and her working as a part-time tutor until the new school year, Esme wasn't in her classroom preparing for school that day. But I knew she still got up early while on summer break.

"You saw him naked?"

"*Mm-hmm.*"

"But there was no sex?"

I shook my head as if she could see me. "None."

"Not even a solicitation to have sex?"

"Nope."

"Okay!" she gushed. "Gentleman."

"Right?!"

I was in my bedroom in my condo. The patio door wide opened giving me the perfect view of Maui at night.

Though the sky outside was dark blue, I could still hear the waves moving along the ocean's surface from my ocean view. Black metal tiki torches all around the resort's grounds lent light to the places around my condo the moon didn't provide.

"I had my titties all out, freshly waxed bikini line in an unobstructed view, and he never made me feel uncomfortable. He didn't make things weird after. We got out of the water, got dressed and completed the hike like he didn't see me with nothing on." I smiled. "Right after, we visited a nearby food truck park, got some food, and ate at one bench while just... talking."

"Hawaii's expensive," I insisted between bites of my Pad Thai.

The food truck owners parked their trucks one in front of the other, forming a giant circle around us. Yusuf and I parked ourselves at the center of the giant circle on a green picnic bench across from each other.

He glanced up at me, cheeks bulging with food, waiting for me to continue.

"You said you've been here several times."

"Okay...?"

I smirked. "I'm trying to find a polite way of asking what in the world do you do where you can afford to visit Maui several times?"

He laughed, covering his mouth with his fist. "You're honest. Nosy, but honest. And oddly... I kind of like that."

I licked my lips of food, and to keep myself from smiling too big, knowing I'd blush if I did.

"I'm a wedding photographer, but I make... well... my wife and I made a bulk of our money as influencers."

My brows piqued.

He smiled to himself. "We're the couple online with the annoying cute videos of us doing annoying cute things and people paying us to do annoying cute things with their products."

"Oh," I commented. "Oh! Wow! That's...really cool."

"It was." He shrugged. "I haven't updated our social accounts in at least a year since she passed, so there have been little sponsorship offers pouring in. And when a few lands in my inbox, I ignore them, for obvious reasons. But once upon a time, uploading videos used to do more than pay our bills. It used to pay our families' bills too. It helped us make a really great living."

"Wow," Esme exhaled. "So, what you guys talk about?"

"Life. Nothing serious. But our talk, as simple as it was, was really nice, Esme. Like, *really* nice."

"Sounds it."

I bit my bottom lip. "He never made me feel uncomfortable, and he never appeared sleazy. Him not making a big deal about the skinny dip was extremely sexy."

"I love that for you, Clarke."

I giggled some more, turning onto my stomach to get a better view outside of my patio.

"So... what's wrong with him?"

"Nothing, except..." I scowled. "He loves his wife."

Esme shouted, "Excuse me?!"

Her shrieking on the other end of my phone almost made me cackle.

"He's a widower."

"Aww, no, what?"

"Yeah. In our talk, he also revealed they were more than a couple. They were business partners. She passed away last year March. He speaks of her so fondly and lovingly. It's enviable if I'm being honest."

"Damn," she whispered. "So... what are *you* trying to do with him, exactly?"

"I… don't know." I laid on my back, eyes up at the ceiling. "I'm here in Maui literally trying to escape any remnants of the unpleasant situation I had with a married emotionally unavailable man, only to find another kind of married emotionally unavailable man to crush on."

"Are you crushing on him?"

"I mean… yeah?"

"Whew, chile."

I hollered a laugh. Esme shared in my humor.

"I shouldn't though, right?"

Esme sighed then said, "You should have fun. You two should enjoy each other's companies. And if things happen… they happen. Just, you know? Set realistic expectations."

I nodded. "Right, yeah."

After a moment with that thought, I shook my head. "No. *Uh-uh.* I *can't.* Plus, I doubt he's thinking about me like that, much less thinking about *anything* happening between us."

"He's still a man, Clarke," Esme reminded. "Even *gentlemen* get aroused and have needs."

"I know, but I…"

… didn't come to Maui for that.

Didn't come here to find a man. As luck would have it, I'd booked this trip an entire year before and when I did, I didn't have in my mind meeting anyone, really. It was a singles' vacation. The prospect of maybe finding something in common with another single crossed my mind, but I was feeling something more than just finding Yusuf interesting. I couldn't get him out of my thoughts and honestly, this feeling started on the plane. And that fact made me a little uncomfortable considering what I'd just dealt with in New York.

"Whatever." I shook my head again, pushing myself up and into a seat on the bed. "Enough about me and all that. How's New York? How are you?"

* * *

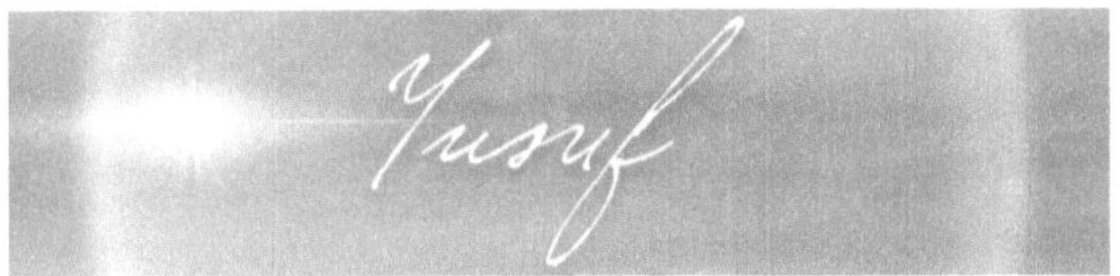

YUSUF

I'm... not okay.

Clarke looked better with her clothes off and frankly, I wasn't prepared for that.

I relaxed in one lounge chair out on my patio, eyes focused straight ahead, studying the shadows of the mountains in the night.

The view was amazing, but the mountain shadows weren't that damn interesting. Staring at them helped me think, though. Helped me process everything that took place that afternoon.

When I got up that morning and skipped the group activity, I did so on purpose and not for the reason I gave Clarke.

I skipped the activity *because* of *her*.

Because as hard as I tried, I couldn't stop my mind from drifting to thoughts about her since I've been here.

Since the flight here, actually. Then again, when I realized she was staying at the same resort as me. Then yet again, when I noticed her in my solo travelers group.

I couldn't shake her.

She just kept popping up. Physically and mentally. Constantly being drawn to wherever I was. It was as if she was some kind of damn magnet...

... that I officially wanted to fuck.

I squeezed my eyes closed at that truth, and slowly ran my hand down my face, hoping to wipe away the feeling.

Because it was a truth, I couldn't escape after that afternoon.

It was a bad idea bringing her to Pua'a Ka'a State Wayside.

A *terrible* idea.

Because that was my wife and I's getaway spot.

Our little secret.

The four times we'd fly to Maui, and we'd visit Pua'a Ka'a State Wayside, Parris and I stopped at the same waterfall hideout to make fresh memories.

To make love.

A gentle breeze blew in from the east, and I closed my eyes to get lost in it and the memory. But the moment I shut my lids; all I could see was Clarke.

Standing there in front of me. Removing her shirt, then wiggling out of her denim shorts and me refusing to blink by the time she reached her arms behind herself to unhook her brown bra.

Her breasts seemed so heavy, spilling out of the lace cups, which wasn't surprising. For a petite woman, she was shapely, not in an over-the-top video vixen kind of way. Just... womanly. Feminine. Soft. Especially her breasts.

I measured C-cup, maybe small D?

My wife Pariss was a full D, and she never shied away from showing them off.

"Good, Yusuf. Think about Parris," I encouraged. "Think only about your wife."

My wife was an affectionate woman. Very sexual, as was I. Our lovemaking only faltered after her brain aneurysm a year prior to her passing. That's when our problems really started.

But before then, we'd make love damn near every single day. Soft and sensual would always turn into hard and rough.

I wonder how Clarke likes it.

I squeezed my eyes shut again, and stood to my feet.

"I need a damn shower," I reasoned with myself.

I needed to cool off.

Bringing Clarke to that waterfall was a bad idea, but I didn't hesitate to do it. I wanted to impress her. Wanted to see what her face looked like lit up with a smile. And I just knew the moment she got an eyeful of one of the rainforest's waterfalls, it would blow her mind, because it blew Parris away the first time we discovered it together.

See? Terrible.

The moment I stepped off the patio and into my bedroom, I lifted the hem of my tee to assist with pulling my shirt up and over my head. I crossed the room in large steps, heading straight for the bathroom, tossing my shirt to the floor, stepping out of my shorts, tossing it, too, and pulling open the shower door to step into the stall.

Lukewarm water cascaded out of the shower head, spraying my skin, and I closed my eyes and stood directly beneath it.

I remembered the look in Clarke's eyes when I removed all my clothes. The shock mixed with arousal in her gaze, but I couldn't be too sure, nor would I explore it.

The sprays of water collided with my skin... and my erection I only noticed from the sensitivity building at the swelling head.

I grunted, dropping my head back.

Frustrated.

Annoyed.

No...

I was disappointed.

Because I couldn't help in that instance but to take my dick into my hand to lull the beast back to sleep. I knew if I didn't, *I* wouldn't get any sleep that night.

My wet hand slid back-and-forth against stiff muscle, gripping the girth tight to speed up the act and get it over with.

But then my mind brought me back to the Pua'a Ka'a State Wayside, trying to see through the clear blue water to glimpse Clarke's body in the nude.

I groaned when I grew stiffer, trying my best to take back my focus, attempting to recollect one of Parris and my many lovemaking sessions.

There was the night after we exchanged vows at City Hall, then our first night in Hawaii.

I licked my lips and gripped harder, slid my hand forth and back faster, squeezing my eyes to hang on to that vision.

The memory of my wife's face contorting in response to me stimulating her with each stroke.

But then Clarke's face faded in, distorting the fantasy.

"*Mmm, fuuuck,*" I drawled, frustrated and defeated when the memory of how Clarke stared at me in the nude created a new fantasy.

So, I gave into it.

I imagined what her mouth would feel like on me. What her pussy would do in reaction to me going deep then deeper.

I pressed a hand flat against the slick tiled wall and increased speed.

She liked to stare. I hoped her intense gazes extended to the bedroom.

Is she a silent lover or loud? Does she caress or scratch? Lick or bite?

My mind filled in the blanks, and the complete picture had me fisting myself now. The wet sounds of me going to work bounced off the bathroom walls along with my deep guttural growls, working myself to the edge.

I was desperate for the nut, panting with each stroke of my palm. Head slung all the way back, teeth clenched and bared, when all I saw was Clarke and what I'd imagined in clear imaging the face she made when she was coming.

Because with me, she would *definitely* come. And I'd make it last to witness her reaction at every phase of her orgasm. Ambitiously, I wouldn't stop until she was boneless.

The muscles in my biceps and forearms quaked. I tried to grip the wall, but I was met with a slippery surface, a throbbing dick, and no idea how I was still standing as the force of it all brought me to the arches of my feet and on my toes as I jerked, spurted, and roared out my release from the depths of my loins.

I had to take a step back to lean the base of my head and the top of my shoulders against the dewy shower door for stability and to catch my breath.

To return to earth.

Because I hadn't felt the need to do that, jerk off, since Parris passed, and I'm concerned in that instance when it isn't enough.

eight

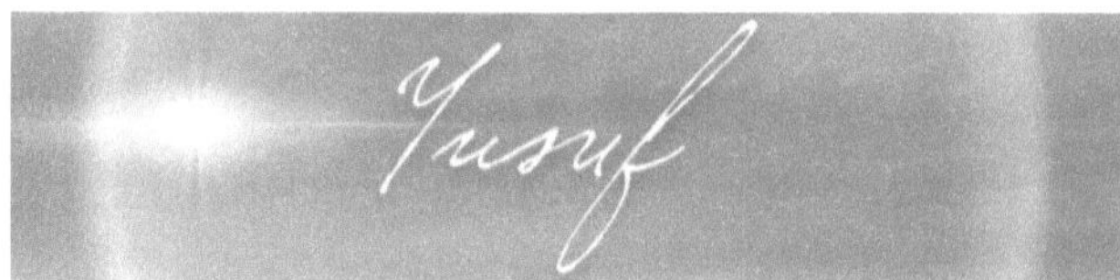

YUSUF

"ATTENTION ISLAND HOP SOLO TRAVELERS, Group A." Patrice shouted from a megaphone. "Charades is starting in ten minutes!"

Clarke was right. This group is boring.

Charades?

Really?

The group's aversion to excitement was the only reason I was looking for Clarke at one of the resort pools.

Well... not the *only* reason.

It was Thursday, late afternoon. The sun was still high, but fading a bit. I slept in that morning having gone to bed late. Spent most of the night masturbating.

Like a horny ass teenager.

To thoughts of Clarke.

I watched familiar faces scatter around me, making their ways to the tent with the Island Hop and HeartMates logos printed along the roof in a monogrammed pattern.

Before the charades activity, there was a sunrise beach visit scheduled for earlier that morning at 5:30 a.m. I didn't finally fall asleep until 4 a.m. But even if I had gotten a full night's rest, I would've skipped the activity. Sunrises weren't my thing. Sunsets were. This was probably one of the few things Parris and I could never agree on because she wasn't a fan of sunsets. She always likened it to endings. But sunrises? She loved them. Would trade sleep in a heartbeat to watch the glow of the sun peek out behind hills as day broke. She loved them anywhere in the world. But absolutely adored them here in Maui.

"Boo!"

The soft brush of Clarke's warm breath on my ear made me skip an exhale. There was a trace of rum in her breath and something else sweet.

She giggled when I turned to face her then she tossed her locs over her shoulders.

If there was a day I needed her not to look the way she looked, it would've needed to be today.

Half of her locs were up while the other half was down. She wore a burnt orange head wrap as a stylish headband. Two locs, one on each side, framed her face.

And I tried to keep my eyes on hers, but I had to do the dumb thing of letting them roam south of her neck to find her very sexy frame barely clothed in a yellow crochet bikini with a matching beach skirt covering her bottom half...

Barely.

"Someone's drunk."

"Tipsy," she corrected, eyes glassy, slightly low-lidded. "And it's a must."

Clarke turned to glance at the tent and gestured towards it. "The only reason I haven't demanded my money back is because I discovered many of the cocktails are free and unlimited here, 24/7." She poked me in the shoulder. "Which you failed to tell me, tour guide!"

I chuckled.

"I am three pina coladas in before 5 p.m. I'm officially in heaven." She licked her lips and took a step towards me, leaning her head back to look up at me. "You missed sunrise."

Her standing beneath me that close, although not *that* close, made blood rush to my dick, making it stiff in my white linen shorts.

She wore light makeup that afternoon. A tinted berry lip gloss that was more clear than colored. And I wanted to mess it all up, leave remnants of it all over my bedsheets.

I cleared my throat and took a step back to create space between us and shared, "I'm more of a sunset guy."

"Oh!" She placed a hand on her narrowed waist. "I don't think they have any sunset activities on the itinerary, which isn't surprising. Everything fun in Maui seems to not make the Island Hop to-go list. As told by charades. Like... what the fuck?"

I snorted a laugh.

"But I'm drunk, so this should be fun."

I laughed this time. "I thought you were tipsy."

She smiled coyly, taking my hand. "Come on."

"Oh, *uh*." I gently removed my hand from hers. Her palm was so soft.

Fuck.

"I... I think I'm going to sit this one out."

Clarke's brows shot up and her eyes ballooned when she told me, "No! No, no, no, no, no."

She had the prettiest mouth.

Clarke's lips weren't as full as Pariss's lips, but they were in the perfect shape. And with her lips damn near forming an O in front of me, it made it easy to imagine what my dick would look like sliding back-and-forth between them.

Stop!

"You will not leave me with them," she contested. "I've had to spend an early morning with them, most of my afternoon. I've resorted to drinking before cocktail hour, for God's sake. It's dire. It's bad. Help. *Me*. Please!"

I hollered a laugh.

"Come play with me, Yusuf." She bit her bottom lip and wiggled her brows.

God, give me the strength.

How could I resist after that?

I couldn't.

And less than a minute later, Clarke and I joined the group for a competitive game of charades.

"Okay, guys!" Patrice said at the front of the tent. Over her shoulder was a view of the ocean. The tides were high, ocean blue, jet skis skating against the water, leaving behind long trails of froth as sunlight reflected along the bubbles. "This game of charades will be the best of five rounds. I know, I know, a quick game. But I don't want to keep you in here all day."

Thank God.

"You'll work in twos and will only have two minutes to guess the title or phrase your partner acts out. You can only use your hands, guys!" Patrice gestured at the bowl on the table in front of her. "When it's your turn, you'll step right up, pick a paper slip out of this bowl, and will act out the title or phrase for your partner to guess. Usually, the rules of charades say that if one team cannot guess the title or phrase, another team can try to guess to steal the point, but we want to keep this succinct, yeah?" She giggled. "So, the first couple to win five points wins the game. And, to make things even more rewarding..." She rubbed her hands together. "The couple who wins the game will win a couple's massage here at the resort!"

"Oh, fuck yeah," Clarke whispered, staring straight ahead. "That's what I'm talking about."

I held back a laugh.

She glanced at me and winked. "You're with me."

Her eyes lingered on me for a second longer until Patrice started talking again.

Those stares.

My God.

I'm still waiting on that strength, God.

There were eight couples paired up in our group, Clarke and I included.

We let the first four go, and they failed terribly, before Clarke and I went up.

Nailed it in less than a minute.

Clarke may have been drunk, but she was sharp.

The final round had us tied with another couple, but they didn't guess the phrase or title before time ran out.

It was Clarke and my turn again. We'd been alternating. Her acting the titles and phrases and me guessing, then me acting and her guessing. For the last go, she would act it out.

She wanted this win and honestly, that was the only reason I gave it my best.

I wanted to see her happy and would do what she wanted to ensure that. That was the first sign I was in danger with this woman.

"Okay," she exhaled, peeking down at the slip again. Clarke licked her lips really slowly, and I had to adjust myself in my seat, because *damn*, I really enjoyed watching her lick her lips. It was my new favorite thing to watch her do. Which, I guess, was another reason we were winning. I wasn't missing a thing, staring at her. Charades gave me an opportunity to gawk, raising no red flags in her head.

Clarke held her hands in front of her face and gestured a stage curtain opening.

"Play," I stated.

She nodded then redid the action but this time pretending to hold a microphone up to her mouth.

"Musical?"

She smiled and nodded again. Licked her lips slowly, this time while thinking.

Got me harder all the same.

She bared her teeth exaggeratively, meowed next, and held her hands at either side of her face, mimicking cat claws.

I knitted my brows. "A cat."

Clarke gestured and nodded, then licked her lips again.

And got me harder once again.

She used her fingers to point at the top of her head, drawing what looked to be a headpiece or a hat.

"Cat hat," I guessed this time. "Cat in the Hat. No." I shook my head. "That's not a musical. *Uhh…. Shit.* Cats?"

She shook her head and gestured at her head again, pointing at the crown of it. Then created a steeple with her fingers on the same spot.

"Crown," I tried this time.

She gestured for me to keep going.

"Queen. King."

Her face lit up with a big smile as she gestured some more.

"Cat king."

She started nodding quickly.

"Cat king," I repeated. My brows shot up. "Lion King?"

"Yes!" Clarke shouted, jumping up and down. "Yes, that's it!"

Patrice hooted and hollered behind Clarke. "You two win!"

Clarke approached, holding her hand up for a high five, which I obliged.

"And you also win a couple's massage, which is set up for you in the resort spa," Patrice added. "Congratulations, you two, and enjoy! You deserved that win. You were amazing and crushed that. Thank you, everyone, for playing!"

* * *

The spa was a huge contrast to charades.

Same ocean view of the waves swelling, undulating, and the shoreline retreating from the sand, only to do it all again.

Soft spa tunes highlighted by the chimes of crystal singing bowls set the vibe as Clark and I laid face down at arm's reach on separate massage tables, naked, and covered from the waist down.

I had to adjust myself repeatedly, hearing her moan in reaction to the masseuse working. I, too, released a few gratifying sounds as my masseuse created tight circles on my skin and along my spine, making her way up to the base of my neck. The moment she got her hands on me, Lani, my masseuse for that session, commented on the bunched-up muscles in my shoulders. I groaned so much as she worked that kink out.

"I'm jealous," Clarke mumbled, a few minutes after our couple's massage session started. "To be so lucky to have that man over there moaning and groaning because of you. Whew. Lucky woman."

I chuckled, recalling her earlier comment.

They had us laid out on the tables for almost an hour when Lani announced, "We are nearing the end of your session, you two."

"Lani, girl, nooo," Clarke whined. "I refuse. What is time, anyway? An illusion."

Lani and I expressed humor at the same time.

"Time is an illusion until it's on a calendar and yours is up." Lani removed her hands from me. "But I can give Yusuf here some pointers on how to give *you* a massage."

I popped my head up at that.

"Oh!" Clarke lifted her head too, to say. "Yusuf and I... We're not..." She chuckled nervously, glancing at me. "That might make things a little uncomfortable..." Clarke focused on me and added, "Right, Yusuf?"

"I don't mind," I confirmed first to Clarke before looking at Lani. "Knowledge is knowledge."

Clarke held a stare with me.

I gestured with my hand in a shrugging motion. "It'll be good for me to learn something new... beyond Maui, is how I see it."

"I mean…" Clarke started. "If… *you* don't mind and it won't make things weird—"

I pushed myself up, pressing my elbows against the table for balance. "It's cool. Promise."

"Awesome," Lani expressed, her already slanted dark eyes slanting deeper as she smiled big. "Yusuf, you can get dressed in the dressing room and when you return, we'll get started. It'll be a quick lesson, swear it."

I was stepping into dangerous territory. Not the dressing room where I quickly changed into my shorts and tee.

Touching Clarke was dangerous as only a thought.

But curiosity had me making my way back to our massage room and my want to hear her moan a little more had me taking my place beside Lani to receive a few pointers on giving a massage.

The basics, of course.

It was only us three in the room now. The masseuse assigned to Clarke, Kaia, left us alone once our session's time ran out.

"Okay." Lani glanced at me and gestured at Clarke's back. "When you are giving a massage, you want to imagine there are tiny dots and arrows scattered along the area your partner would like you to massage in an organized pattern. Your job is to use the pads of your fingertips to rub those dots and arrows out."

I nodded my understanding.

Lani rolled the white draping covering Clarke's naked body low enough to expose Clarke's slender back.

And what a nice back it was.

Clarke's ass formed a small mountain beneath the draping and I had to force my eyes to the top half of her mound, peeking below the draping's hemline.

I've always loved a good mountain view.

"If we were working on you, Yusuf." Lani smiled, regaining my attention. "We would focus more on your back, neck, and shoulders since men like yourself, big, strong, and brawny…"

I smiled back.

"... feel the tensest in those areas and tightness in those spots result in headaches near your cervical spine." Lani placed a hand below my neck. "Right here."

"Got ya."

"But with Clarke, you're going to focus your attention *here*." Lani gently placed a hand on Clarke's lower back.

Clarke moaned at Lani's touch. "Don't make me fall for you, Lani."

Lani giggled, and I chuckled.

"Yusuf." Lani held her hand in a cupping shape. "Cup your fingers like this."

I did as demonstrated.

Lani took me by the wrist, poured a little warm coconut oil into my palm, and placed my oiled fingers at the base of Clarke's lower back.

"Rock your hand back and forth like so. Gently."

Clarke's skin was so soft and warm against my hand. She felt nice.

Really nice.

"Make sure your back is straight and you keep your head leveled as it is, so you don't strain your lower back while giving a lower back massage to your partner. How ironic would that be?"

I was too distracted to react with words or even a sound of humor.

Clarke breathing heavy beneath me in reaction to me touching her was more my interest.

"Okay, we have time for one more lesson. Clarke," Lani said, lowering her eyes to Clarke. "I'm going to teach Yusuf how to massage your quads. Is that fine?"

"Fine with me." Clarke lifted her neck and then turned her head to focus up at me. "You cool with it?"

Her lids were low. Sexy low. I had to force myself to nod because words would not come out of my damn mouth.

She had me a little spellbound.

Lani took one side of the draping in her grip. "I'll hold the draping to keep you covered as you turn over onto your back."

Once Clarke was in position, on her back and lying face up, Lani adjusted the white draping, placing the hem of one end over Clarke's private area, revealing one of her slim, thick thighs to me while covering the other.

My eyes moved off it to Clarke to see her looking right at me before allowing a smile to pull at her lips.

I pushed my tongue against my cheek to keep from smiling back.

Which was a lost cause.

"Now with your partner's legs," Lani started. "And Clarke, this will be helpful for you to know as well, so listen up."

"Oh," Clarke chimed in. "I'm present professor."

Lani snickered, glancing up at me. "She's very funny."

I peeked down at Clarke and said, "Hilarious."

Clarke licked her lips slow.

"Stop," I mouthed.

That made Clarke giggle.

"With legs, effleurage and crab claw massage techniques work best. Crab claw is exactly how it sounds. Four fingers closing to meet the pad of your thumb. Effleurage is as easy." Lani pressed her hand against Clarke's thigh. "A continuous circular stroking motion."

"Stroking," Clarke repeated.

I shook my head, biting back a smile.

Lani had just finished showing me how to squeeze and shake to massage Clarke's quad and was preparing to show me how to execute a petrissage when we were interrupted by another masseuse.

"My apologies but Lani," the short-haired woman stated. "You have a call at the front desk. It's the suppliers again."

"Oh! I must take this. Thank you, Lolana." Lani glanced at me, then at Clarke. "I'll be only a moment but Yusuf, while I'm gone, practice the effleurage technique I showed you earlier against Clarke's quads."

I looked at Clarke.

"I'll only be a minute," Lani promised, exiting the room and closing the door behind herself.

Clarke and I were alone. Her naked and covered from her chest to her feet with only a thigh exposed. I fully dressed.

For the first few seconds, I stood there doing nothing.

Until Clarke stated, "Well...you heard her. Let's see what you've learned."

I swallowed hard, looking at her thigh.

"All right." I grabbed the bottle of coconut oil, squirted a translucent nickel-sized amount into my palm, and rubbed my hands together, warming the oil, as Lani taught me.

Cleared my throat when I approached Clarke again and laid one palm at the top of her soft thigh and another hand on the spot I planned to massage.

I moved my hand in a circular stroking motion, as advised, watching Clarke's chest rise and fall as her eyes closed.

I asked low, "Is that good?"

"*Mm-hmm*," she moaned.

The higher up her thigh I moved to massage, she'd moan deeper and the whole thing was making me stiffen again.

I kept my physical attention on her thigh most of the time, so when I finally moved my eyes off her leg to check her expression, she was staring up at me with sultry eyes.

Low lids feathered by long lashes.

Barely blinking.

I felt her leg move apart from its original position. I glanced down there, then back at her.

She looked me right in my eyes, licked her lips really slowly as she slid her thighs even farther apart.

I narrowed my eyes at her, catching the hint, but still not too sure I was picking up what she was throwing down.

Consent?

It had been a year since I was intimate with a woman, but even *I* could read a green light.

So... I went for it.

I slid my hand farther up her inner thigh until my fingertips detected wet heat.

Her breathing became heavier. She slid her thighs even farther apart.

I glanced at her again, and she nodded slowly.

"It's okay," she whispered. "You can touch me."

I relaxed my brows at that and moved my fingers beneath the white draping. She bit her bottom lip and closed her eyes as I brushed my fingertips against shaven lower lips.

"*Mm-hmm*," she encouraged. She swallowed hard and told me, "Keep going, Yusuf."

If I wasn't hard before, I was rock hard now. And you would think that would snap me out of whatever moment was happening between us in that massage room with my hand now pressed against the shape of Clarke's warm pussy, but it did no such thing.

It inspired me to do exactly what she told me to do.

Keep going.

But deeper.

I moved slowly, sliding my fingertips up her wet slit, applying the right amount of pressure to part her lower lips in my search for her clit.

"*Mm-hmm*," she encouraged again, nodding this time while spreading her thighs wider now.

And when my index and middle fingers found her smooth pink ball, she and I both shared a moan at my discovery.

I created slow tight circles along the surface, pressing the ridged underside of my finger's joint against the very tip of her bundle of nerves to increase sensitivity, a technique I knew would drive Clarke wild...

... Because it used to have the same effect on Parris.

Clarke was so wet against my fingertips. I was throbbing in my shorts when I moved in closer to the table to press my free hand against her abdomen to keep her still when she began writhing against my palm.

"Easy," I whispered, really wanting to whisper that in her ear with me buried to the hilt inside her. "Am I making you feel *that* good?"

"Yes," she panted, arching her back off the table and gyrating her hips against my fingers now.

"*Mmm*, I love hearing that." I moaned along with her, briefly checking over my shoulder at the closed door. "And I love hearing you. But you have to keep it down for me. Okay, Clarke?"

"Okay," she whimpered.

"Unless..." I slowly slid two fingers inside her and adjusted my wrist. Used my thumb to continue massaging her pink ball as I curved my fingers up at the knuckles. "... unless you *want* them to hear you."

She sucked in air then tucked her pretty lips into her mouth to bite them closed.

"Do you want me to make them hear you?" I circled her clit faster, massaged her g-spot with the same speed. "I can if you want me to."

She moaned louder, and I groaned in response.

"Tell me what you want, Clarke," I exhaled. "I swear I'll give you anything you want sounding like *this*."

Her eyes opened to mine, hips still gyrating, body trembling, walls quivering, neither one of us stopping what we were doing when she told me, "I want you to fuck me."

The room's door swung open, and I pulled my hand back just as fast. I moved closer to the table to hide my hard-on, trying to poke a hole through my shorts.

Shit!

"I am *so* sorry," Lani announced, reentering the room.

I looked to Clarke to see her panting heavily and adjusting the draping over her lower body.

Her wetness on my fingers was testing my resilience, not to clean her essence off my fingertips with my tongue.

"That was one of our suppliers calling, trying to sort out one of our delayed orders. We've been playing phone tag all morning and…" Lani waved her hand in the air. "You don't care about *any* of that, nor should you."

Clarke looked at me, and I did at her, too.

The look in her eyes was undeniable.

Her words were intelligible.

She wanted what I wanted.

And there was no doubt about it now.

"So." Lani pressed a hand to my arm and focused down on Clarke. "How was he?"

"Amazing." Clarke said with more breath than tone. "That…" She pressed her hand to her chest to gather her next words. "Lani, that was the *best* massage I've ever had in my life. No offense to Kaia. But Yusuf, *mmmm*." She blew air through her lips. "He got them hands, girl."

I smiled while shaking my head.

I guess that strength will not show up, huh?

Because it wasn't a question of *if* Clarke and I would hook up while here in Maui.

It was more so a wonder *when* it would happen… and if I would let it.

CLARKE

SO... *that* happened.

And I couldn't blame it all on the liquor.

I lounged on my patio, the ocean breeze blowing in from straight ahead. I guided my attention across the resort's grounds from my view next. My eyes roamed over one of the resort pools and then the monogrammed tent Yusuf and I were under with the rest of our group playing charades earlier.

Little did we know what would happen after we won that innocent game.

I shut my eyes, slightly embarrassed, very aroused, at what occurred only an hour prior.

That man made me orgasm on those people's massage table.

And I let him do it.

I facepalmed myself while giggling.

I thought against going through with it when the idea first popped into my head. His hand on my thigh had my body tingling, and the little rum still coursing through my veins, plus that vacay brand of energy pulsing through me, encouraged me to part my legs.

Did I think he'd go for it?

Not really.

Shocked me a little, he did.

Excited me a lot, he didn't stop until he fingered an orgasm out of me.

He made me come on that table while knuckles deep!

And was *so* calm about it.

Which was even more of a turn on.

Yusuf was so attentive to my every reaction.

And the things he said to me...

He was giving all the signs he was a self-contained beast in bed.

The wanting to know if what he was doing was making me feel good had me losing my mind.

And if he could make my body do that with only his hands, what earth-shattering kiss-the-sky-pleasure could he help me reach with his dick?

And gosh, that dick...

His dick was so hard when Lani left the room for good. This was after she returned to the room following her longer than expected phone call. I watched him palm his erection a few times to get it to relax, and I wanted to help bury it somewhere warm. And even when he had his own thing to get under control, he was still checking on me. As always, a gentleman.

"You good?" He asked, gripping and releasing his stiffness, not real-izing he was turning me on again, only doing that.

I swung my legs off the table to sit up on it.

I was in love at that point.

Well, maybe not love, but the brother had me floating somewhere in the clouds like I was.

"I'm great."

He held out a hand, not the one he made me come with. The one he's been trying to relax his hard-on with, and he helped me step down off the table.

My legs, as expected, could barely hold me up, but he was there to catch me.

"It was like that?" He queried with a smirk.

I inhaled a deep breath and let it out as a sigh. "And more."

He stepped out of the massage room for me to get dressed after, which I thought was unnecessary since he'd already seen me naked.

But... he's a gentleman, and that's what gentlemen do.

And I wanted to disrupt that a little. Get him out of his element. At least after he talked me through my orgasm the way he did.

I likened it to a man finding pleasure in ruining a woman's perfect appearance.

You know? Smearing her lipstick.

Sweating out her perfectly laid edges.

I wanted to see him get messy for once.

Composure was Yusuf's brand.

Composed when he saw me naked, composed when he saw my come face. Just always calm and composed.

And beyond wanting him to fuck me, which I confessed while climaxing, I wanted to see him crack... in a good way.

I wonder what his wife was like.

My not-so-random thought didn't remain a wonder for long.

Because shortly after I had it, I was reaching for my device to tap into my socials to do a little... research.

When we were in the food truck lot the day prior, Yusuf shared with me the social handle he and his wife used for their accounts. And my paralegal brain wouldn't let me forget it.

I was on their social page faster than I could type in the first four letters of their handle. My jaw dropping soon after.

The first thing I noticed was the follower count. He said he and his wife were influencers.

But to 240,000 people?

"Oh my God."

The way he explained it – him and his wife used their account as a hobby that paid well. Recording cutesy videos of themselves being themselves and uploading them.

But he didn't tell me how many people were interested in that. And many were. Thousands of them were, in fact.

And he also failed to tell me how absolutely *adorable* the two of them were together.

She was beautiful.

No. Stunning.

With a dark pixie cut she wore slicked down most of the time and light eyes that were more beautiful, not because of the light brown color, but because of the amount of light sparkling in them.

Parris.

Her name was Parris, and it was the most perfect name for a beautiful woman.

And she wasn't only beautiful in the eyes. Her beauty was an inside job, too.

From the first three videos I allowed sound on, she was effervescent and full of life. Spunky and funny. And a bit of a menace with her clever yet slightly devilish pranks. She was clearly more of the on-camera type. Her beautiful face appeared in most of their account's thumbnail photos.

And he loved her... a lot. Every video uploaded, and that they recorded together, Yusuf was smiling from ear to ear. He looked different, laughing from his diaphragm to the point of tears.

He was happy.

Jubilant.

There was one video that made my breathing cease. Recorded with long stalks of bright green bamboo in the backdrop as they filmed themselves, sharing a kiss with the sound of a waterfall cascading into a pool of water behind them.

I started breathing heavy, my heavy heart sinking to the bottom of that pool.

I knew the place. He took me there.

It was *their* spot.

He shared as much in the video, smiling bigger than I've ever seen him smile with me.

I placed my phone flat on my lap when the thought crossed my mind.

Of course, he smiled bigger at her. She was his wife. And he loved her with everything in him. It was abundantly clear he loved her that much, likely even more than he showed.

"Damn," I whispered, leaning my head against the lounge chair's headrest.

I would've liked her. I would've loved *them*.

Yusuf was a good husband. He was great. Not for the camera, although that's all I had to go off. But in the two personal videos I watched of them simply documenting their lives, he genuinely looked happy to be married. And it was refreshing.

Like social proof.

That there was a man in this world who genuinely loved being married to his wife.

And in that moment, I felt both blessed and cursed.

Blessed in finding a great man who had a good heart. And cursed because I would probably never have that good heart of his, even if I wanted it... because his fantastic heart still belonged to his amazing deceased wife.

ten

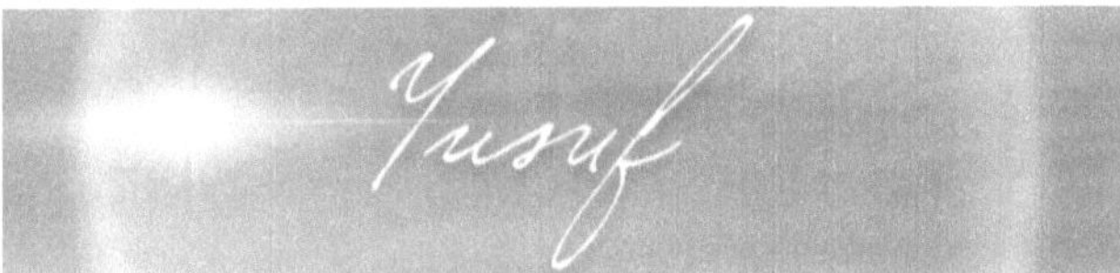

YUSUF

I TAPPED my finger on the console table's surface and stared down at my condo's phone.

For another night in a row, I spent most of the time masturbating to the point of exhaustion and waking the next morning later than usual because of that.

All thoughts centered on Clarke, of course.

I was officially deep in that rabbit hole.

Speaking of deep...

I could still smell her on my hand, on my fingers. And yes, I'd washed my hands. I wasn't a creep. But in my mind, her essence would remain on my fingertips for as long as I could remember our time at the spa.

On an early afternoon on a Friday, I was standing over the console table with the room phone, contemplating calling her room.

As a group member in Island Hop's solo travelers group, we were all required to leave our full names and room numbers at concierge. Took some convincing to get the concierge to share with me Clarke's room number, for security reasons, of course. But when I told her my sincere intentions for simply wanting to call Clarke on her room phone, the concierge couldn't resist and gave it to me.

There was a reggae dance party our group had scheduled for later that night. It would be the first party event for our group and, according to Patrice, we would be joined by the other Island Hop group, Group B, giving us more opportunity to mingle with fresh faces.

But I honestly didn't care for anyone else besides Clarke.

Shouldn't have been caring for her at all, if I'm being honest.

But I did.

Couldn't get her moans off my mind or how she looked giving in to me.

It was nothing like I imagined. The actual moment was astronomically better.

But I wanted more when I shouldn't have wanted it at all, and here I was standing over the console table, considering calling her. To put us in the same place on purpose this time for once.

I lifted the cordless phone off its base and keyed in her room number, listening to the line trill twice before she answered with, "Hello?"

"Clarke, hey."

There was silence for a beat before she asked, "Yusuf?"

She sounded good on the phone. Even better, saying my name in my ear. Sounded so good I couldn't help but to smile to myself.

"Yeah, it's me." I nodded. "How are you?"

"Cheesing so hard my face hurts. You?"

I chuckled.

"Calling me now?"

"Calling you now," I confirmed.

"I have to say," she started. "I am flattered, because I know it wasn't easy getting my room number to get in touch with me."

"Thank you for noticing."

"You sound good on the phone," she complimented in a whisper. "Very sexy."

"Ditto."

We were silent for a moment before I added, "And although I love how you sound on the phone, that's not the reason I'm calling."

"Oh?"

I bit my bottom lip, then released it. "You've seen the sunrise and I think it's only fair you at least see one sunset. They're better."

"Are they?"

"Very much so."

"Do you have any recommendations where I can see at least one?"

"I'll do you one better," I told her. "I'll take you."

"Really?" she asked softly.

"*Mm-hmm.*" I peeked down at my wristwatch. "Sunsets in Maui typically happen around 7:15 p.m. Meet me in the lobby at 4:30 p.m. so we can head out and catch it in time. It takes about three hours to drive up to the highest point in Maui."

"Three hours?"

"Yeah." I bit at my lip, a little nervous. "Is that fine?"

"It's great," she assured. "I'm sure it will be worth it, so okay, will do."

"It'll definitely be worth it," I promised. "Bring a sweater or blanket if you have it."

"A sweater or blanket? Why?"

"Believe it or not, where I'm taking you will be cold." I smiled, excited to return to one of my favorite places in Maui. "You'll need something to keep warm."

* * *

"Like…" Clarke started. "Are we still on planet earth right now?"

I snickered to myself in my seat on the hard surface next to her. It was exactly 7:10 p.m. and the sun was beginning its descent behind the clouds.

We were literally at the top of Maui. High enough to see the entire island.

"Just wow," she breathed, glancing at me. Clarke covered her shoulders in the coral throw blanket she brought with her from her condo. "We literally have our heads in the clouds."

I chuckled and nodded. "Literally."

We were in Haleakala National Park, home to the Haleakala shield volcano. Clarke and I, along with other sunset observers, were at Maui's highest point, sitting over 10,000 feet above the ground.

I decided to rent a car from a tiny local rental lot a mile from the resort. The lot was owned by a young couple who were so grateful for our business. The visit to Haleakala was too far out of the way for any of the resort's shuttles, so a rental was needed.

The drive up here was easy.

Clarke and I stopped at a roadside stand known as Hana Farms on the way to the park. The roadside stand and restaurant had a few goodies, like banana bread and candy nuts I believed would be good to snack on while we rode up to Haleakala's visitor's center to park our rental. I figured eating as I drove would add to the experience and distract us long enough not to realize the time it took to drive up to the top.

"You weren't lying when you said it was cold up here," she wrapped the blanket more around herself. "It feels like a New York winter this high up."

"It's about thirty-nine degrees, so that's about right."

She shook her head, eyes returning to the sun slowly dipping underneath the horizon. "It's so bizarre, you know? It's like… we left earth and are on another planet somewhere in outer space. Some-where freezing yet beautiful with craters. I am literally sitting in the clouds, on a volcanic mountain, engulfed in fog, and I'm in absolute heaven."

I smiled to myself.

I knew she'd love it.

"You were right." She swooned. "This is *way* better than a sunrise."

"Right?!" I whispered. "Wait until the sun has completely set and you get a look at the night sky." I bit my bottom lip. "You'll *never* be the same after you see it."

She giggled. "I believe you."

We were quiet for a few before she asked, "How do you know all these cool places in Maui, anyway?"

I shrugged. "I'm a wedding photographer who had clients who couldn't stop talking about going on their incredible honeymoons in Hawaii. You hear about the great places to visit enough times to go look them up yourself to experience them too."

She nodded then asked, "Did you used to bring Parris here when you two visited the island?"

I turned my head to meet her eyes. "You know her name."

A statement, not a question.

"But how?" I added. "I've never told you—"

"I was being a creep last night." She cringed, and dropped her head into her hand. "I looked you up. Looked you two up. Your social page on IG."

I made a shrugging motion with the corners of my mouth.

"Which," she continued with a brow raised. "240,000 followers, Yusuf?"

I let a little laugh leave my lips.

"My guy." Clarke leaned forward to look me in my eyes. "You failed to tell me you are internet famous."

"Was," I corrected. "I… haven't updated that page or any of our other social pages since announcing Parris's passing."

"I noticed," she whispered. "Yusuf."

I looked her way.

"She was beautiful."

I took a breath to keep my emotions in and not have them roll down my cheeks.

Because she was. Parris was a light you always wanted to get close to.

At least I did.

Clarke shook her head. "She was… so beautiful. Not of this world, beautiful."

"*That…*" I whispered. "That is the perfect way to describe her." I nodded, eyes staring off into the distance to keep myself from breaking. "Sincerely."

The sun had fully set, leaving behind a denim blue sky with specs of silver dots for rivets slowly fading in along the sky's surface.

It was like being in a planetarium, watching the sky transform before my eyes.

"My therapist keeps telling me to update my pages. He's been recommending I do it for months. Not for updating our followers. For closure."

I shook my head.

"But I doubt I'll ever do that. Too much pain. Too many memories."

"It was you and your wife's thing," Clarke added. "I get it."

"Yeah," I concurred low.

"Yusuf."

Her tone was the same apologetic tone she had with me the day I revealed I was a widower. The low somberness. The upturn of my name to hint that something more was coming after she said it.

"I feel like," she started, "we should address what happened at the spa yesterday."

I tried to suppress my smile, but couldn't. I refused to anyway because it was the sudden relief I needed from feeling down again, thinking about Parris.

Clarke felt like we should address what happened at the spa and there hasn't been a moment I haven't been addressing it in my head.

"I had a lot to drink yesterday."

"I didn't," I clarified.

"But I..." She cleared her throat. "I seduced you."

I laughed. "Clarke."

"What?" she questioned. "What's funny?"

"It's so *cute* you think you seduced me."

She looked at me with a slacked jaw, then scoffed a laugh. "Well, there goes my ego."

"Please don't take it like that." I turned to look her right in the eyes to tell her, "What I mean is, everything that happened, I *wanted* to happen."

"You loved your wife—"

"I *love* her," I corrected. "And I always will. Nothing will change that."

She and I held a stare.

"And... I'd be lying if I didn't acknowledge that, despite what happened at the spa, I still love my wife *very* much."

Clarke nodded.

"But you..." I bit my bottom lip and smiled. "You make me remember a time when life was exciting, carefree, and not so damn sad, Clarke. When grief wasn't so threaded in my identity. When adventure was an actual pulse in my life. A pulse that has been flatlining for an entire year. And in six days, I found it and the air is easier to breathe again. You helped me do that from the moment you insulted me on the flight over here."

"Oh, gosh—"

I laid a hand on hers. "And I wouldn't have wanted you to change a thing because then you would change what I really like about you. What I like a lot. So, *please*, keep being Clarke. 'Cause I like her as she is."

She smiled.

"We're here in Maui, for our own reasons. Let's just... be *here*." I nodded to myself. "What happened at the spa happened. It was beautiful. It was sexy. It was an experience I can't stop thinking about and honestly... I would much rather think about what happened at the spa instead of thinking about the things that make me sad. So, there. We talked about it."

I glanced at the view in front of us, which was all black sky and silver stars, and gestured with my chin. "Let's talk about *that*."

Clarke gasped, and pressed her hand to her chest.

"Yeah," I expressed, feeling my heart fill with so many emotions I wouldn't dare put words to. "I know."

* * *

Clarke and I arrived at the Island Hop reggae dance party shortly after the event started.

After returning the rental to the young Hawaiian couple, Clarke and I split up to head back to our condos to freshen up and change into our outfits for the party. We met up again in the resort's lobby and walked to the party together.

They held the party outside on a sectioned-off part of the resort's private beach. A line of tiki torches lit up the area and added to the laid-back island feel of the event.

Reggae dancehall music echoed from speakers set up inside a tent. A DJ lifted and dropped his turntable needle onto the vinyl he just set down, wedging one muff of his headphones between his head and his shoulder.

Clarke and I made our way to the bar setup upon arrival and that's where we remained for at least half an hour until...

"Whewww!" Clarke shouted, closing her eyes and swaying from left to right on her barstool. "This is my song!"

We were at least two Mai Tais in each. While I took my time sipping mine, Clarke wasted no time gulping hers. I realized Clarke was a happy drunk. Not to say she was drunk. But she was definitely feeling... something other than sober. And by the time I could see the bottom of my glass, I was feeling something too.

Her perfectly rolled locs were down tonight and laying against her shoulders. Clarke's skin glowed beneath the moonlight and the tiki torches. She wore a burnt orange dress with ruffle-like sleeves. Her dress clung to every one of her curves and stressed the shape of her breasts. They were straining against the fabric.

It seemed the reggae track was everyone's favorite because the area sectioned-off for dancing gradually filled with people when it was empty less than a minute prior to the song playing.

Clarke squealed next, jumping to her feet. She reached across me for her drink and tossed the rest into her mouth.

She was reaching for my hand as she gulped the last of it.

"Let's go dance."

"Wh-what?" I asked, eyes bouncing between her and the dance area. "Nah."

"Oh, come on." She circled her hips in slow motion to the exotic rhythm in the song in front of me. "You don't feel that?"

Oh, I was feeling something.

"I'm not much of a dancer," I admitted to her hips.

She used her grip on my chin to lift my head so our eyes met.

"Just stand there then." She winked. "I'll handle the rest."

When she pulled on my hand a second time, I rose to my feet and let her guide me into the crowd. We quickly found our place in the mix.

Similar to at the bar, Clarke rocked her hips from left to right in front of me, turning every so often to dance with her back facing me. Pulled me close, then closer, until the only thing that could pass between us were the dirty thoughts her ass on me was eliciting.

She'd turned to face me when she screamed over the song, "And you said you couldn't dance. You seem to move to the song just fine."

"I didn't say I couldn't dance," I clarified. "I said I'm not a dancing guy."

She smiled slyly, turning to rock her ass against me, guiding my hand to her waist to hold on. The feel of her up against me was satisfying wants I didn't even know I could have with someone I knew for only six days.

Throughout the duration of the reggae dance party on the beach, we laughed, caused each other's pulse to race. Well, at least Clarke caused mine to race like crazy.

She moved to each song that played like she was the beat. Oscillating her hips around and around, closing her eyes as if she were making love to the lyrics in each song. I wasn't a dancing kind of guy by any measure, but I swear, I'd stay right there with her for as long as she wanted.

Because the cosmic exchange between us was life-giving. What she was giving me in return was a gift...

A chance to breathe again.

The ocean in the distance, filling the air with the scent of salt water and under a night sky, visual artists often tried to recreate in paintings... I felt like me again.

It was bittersweet.

But the night was young, and I allowed myself to feel that young energy pumping in my heart. More interested in creating more feelings like *this*, another distraction, and I was happy... even though I knew my happiness couldn't possibly last.

eleven

CLARKE

"*I WILL TAKE the stars out the sky for you...*" I sang off-key, dancing toward my condo's door, humming the rest of the Mya and Beenie Man lyrics from "Girls Dem Sugar."

I heard Yusuf chuckling low from not far behind me. I spun his way to sing the last of the lyrics to him and lost my footing for only a moment before he was there to catch me with one arm.

"Whoa." He chuckled more, stumbling forward but getting us both in balance. His eyes were a little less glassy than mine. "You might have had too much to drink."

"I didn't have enough," I joked, pressing a hand to his chest.

The night was incredible. Like, truly incredible and life altering for the best.

The trip to the park to watch the sunset was a kind of intimacy

I've never experienced. And I'm not talking about the amazing company Yusuf was to me. It was his idea to rent the red Toyota from a local couple to drive to the top of a volcano to watch the sun bid farewell for the day.

The intimacy was in being introduced to a different way to get in touch with reality. For the first time in days, I wasn't thinking about working at the law office. I didn't bog my mind down remembering being betrayed or feeling stupid for not seeing the signs of being involved with a married man.

High on that shield volcano with only the sun, the clouds, and my inhales and exhales, nothing else mattered. My mind was finally quiet. And seeing the stars gradually light up the sky like loose melee diamonds, shimmering without me doing nothing but sitting there, was phenomenal.

I was feeling... alive.

I regained my balance and gently pulled away from Yusuf. My attention landed on big thick arms and a hard chest kept contained in a gray and white Hawaiian floral printed shirt with a hem that hung over white hoochie daddy shorts.

Thank you Juliette for teaching your girl the cut of those shorts way back when.

He wore it so well.

Yusuf's outfit appeared tailored to him. A perfect fit.

I loved his style, and not just his style of dress. The way he carried himself. With patience and reserve... and loyalty. Yusuf made my body do things with only his fingers, made me feel like the only woman he had eyes for and used those same eyes to tell me, though what we experienced was amazing, he still loved his wife.

And nothing would change that.

I was in admiration after he set the situation straight.

Because... *wow.*

The existence of a man, ladies and gentlemen.

A real man.

I felt like I needed to plant a flag on him. To prove the existence of an actual good man on planet earth. To let the record show, he was here and there had to be more like him. So other women would know like I learned we didn't have to lose hope or settle for mediocrity, convinced the selection of liars, cheaters, misogynistic man children were the best we could do so we better pick through what's available before our time was up. Because there was a man walking this earth who loved and respected his wife in death in the same capacity, he loved and respected her in life.

And that shit? Was *so* sexy.

I had to have some of that... even if it was for only one night.

"Here we are," I announced when we were feet away from my condo's front door.

I was in front of it when I turned to face Yusuf. He stood at a comfortable distance... for him. A roadside stand similar to the one we stopped at before arriving at the park for sunset could fit comfortably between us.

We stood there for a moment, saying and doing nothing.

"Okay." He nodded once. "Goodnight... Clarke."

Yusuf turned his perfect toes in his flip-flops to head towards the way we came from when I asked, "Do you want to come in?"

He looked at me like I'd broken a commandment asking my question. A mix of shock and intrigue because we both knew what him coming inside meant. So maybe I broke some kind of commandment. At the very least, a virtue? And maybe I shouldn't have been feeling what I was feeling for a bereaved man. Yusuf spoke of his wife like she was a saint and, based on their videos on their social page, the title saint wasn't a far off one.

But...

What he said to me at the park? About how I reminded him about the excitement of life and how I helped him feel like him again?

I kind of felt vindicated from guilt for wanting a man who still loved his dead wife.

"I..." he started, "I think I should go back to *my* room."

"Aren't you curious about the ocean view?"

Whew. The desperation.

"I remember you saying you booked the mountain view."

He smirked. "I know what the ocean view looks like, Clarke. We stayed in a condo with one at least once."

We.

Not Parris and me.

Just, we.

That helped a lot, not hearing him say her name.

"But you've never seen it with me."

Yusuf stared at me for two breaths before looking away to swallow hard and take a step back.

"Clarke," he said low. "We've been drinking… you're drunk—"

"Drunk behavior is sober thoughts," I imparted even lower.

His hesitance should've made me recoil. It should have made me decide against pushing my back off my door to make my way over to him.

But it didn't. It made me want him more than before.

Close, I pressed a hand to his chest, feeling as his heart hammered against my palm through his Hawaiian shirt. You wouldn't even tell all of that was happening inside of him with how calm he looked and how even his expression was with me standing only inches away from him.

"I don't normally do this," I revealed to him. "I don't pursue."

He licked his lips slowly.

"But I've never experienced such a pull to a man, the way I feel with you, *ever* in my life."

I walked closer and stood under him. His warm exhales brushed against the very fine hairs on my face, elevating the heat in me, causing my pulse to race.

"You have every right to say no to me, and I'll respect your choice if that is where you remain with my invite tonight."

He blinked in response.

"But I've already confessed to wanting you." I licked my lips menacingly slow. "And since that short time, that want has only intensified. 'Cause now? I want you so bad Yu—"

My last word to him barely made it out of my mouth before Yusuf grabbed me by the back of my head to pull me close so he could crash his lips into mine.

The move took me completely off guard. Obviously, it was what I was working toward happening. I was damn near telling the man to come into my room and have his way with me in fewer words, but the switch up... it was a plot twist in the moment that literally brought me to my toes to stay in it.

He backed me toward my door and skillfully removed my key card from my hand. I imagined he waved the card in front of the censor because the sound of the door unlocking and the weight of it giving way behind me let me know he'd gotten it open.

I tasted the Mai Tai on his tongue and traces of the candy nuts we snacked on at the back of the resort's shuttle. His lips covered mine completely, leaving no room for me to moan.

To breathe.

Because his kiss was orgasmic.

No exaggeration.

No lie.

He was fucking me with his tongue, and I sincerely believed I could come like that. I *really* wanted to see if I could.

Our kissing didn't stop or lose heat the moment my sandals' soles touched the shiny stone floors in my condo. It didn't falter when he bent his legs at the knees to lift me, to carry me into my bedroom.

The ocean's waves rippling underneath the moonlight were louder in my room than the living area because of the reduce cubic feet of space in my bedroom and it was an excellent substitute to our kissing.

Yusuf placed me on the console table far beneath the mounted flatscreen, then kissed himself off my lips.

He glanced down at us. Me there with my legs splayed wide to accommodate him standing between them. My dress hiked up enough to reveal thighs but still too low to show his prize.

He shook his head, out of breath, and said, "I don't have... we don't have any..."

"Condoms?" I panted.

I reached for the Island Hop welcome bag I found in the condo when I arrived days ago, pushing my hand into it and throwing everything that didn't feel like a tiny box onto the floor until I got the box in hand.

I held the box of magnums up in his view.

Ripped it open a second later when I noticed he hadn't reached for the box. With a wrapped condom singled out and placed beside my right thigh, I lifted myself high enough to slide my lace panties off.

Yusuf seemed in a daze. Frozen in place. I had trouble making room between us to remove my underwear.

But I managed to wiggle out of them because, *duh*, fine man standing in front of me, right?

And no doubt worth the extra effort.

I held the single condom up for him to take, but he wouldn't.

He just stared at it.

Any sane woman would know that maybe she should course correct. The look on his face was one of disbelief. Shock. Sort of blank. Void of emotion, but still so intense.

My crazy ass found it intriguing.

Challenging.

And maybe I was being selfish. Ignorant and selfish to the gravity of the moment, he was having standing between the legs of a woman who wasn't his wife.

But respectfully... she was gone. I was here. And for once, I wanted to think only about Clarke and what she wanted guilt-free.

And she wanted Yusuf, dammit!

I raised the wrapped condom to my lips and his eyes followed my action. I held the edge of the gold wrapper to my teeth and bit down, ripping the packaging opened.

Wrapped my legs around his waist and used them to pull Yusuf closer to me. And he allowed me to close the distance between us. I pressed the back of my shoulders to the wall behind the console table to slide my lower half closer to him. His Adam's apple bobbed as he swallowed in reaction to me, lifting the hem of his shirt to access the button on his shorts.

The whole time he said nothing, and I didn't either. We communicated through heavy breaths and unwavering eye contact and the entire thing was a turn on I never knew I could achieve.

He inhaled deeply when I pushed my hand slowly into his shorts, then his boxer briefs to pull out his dick.

And he was hard, which brought a smirk to my lips that I suppressed.

He was hard for me.

That was great.

It was encouraging to see too.

I gripped my hand around his hardness and jerked him off slowly, watching as his chest heaved up and down.

And when I felt the time was right, I removed the slick condom from its wrapper and slid it down his hard-on.

Covered, I slid closer, only stopping when the head of his dick poked against my lower lips.

My lids lowered a little when I took him again in my hand to run his sheathed erection up and down my slit. Biting my bottom lip and circling my hips at the feel of him, watching the look in his eyes transition from shock to desire.

Desire contained, but palpable, between us.

Yusuf gripped me by my hips to still me as he pushed his way inside of me.

My jaw dropped, feeling my walls give way.

His head dropped back between his shoulders as he sipped the air, hissing through his teeth as he inched his way in. Groaning softly after in reaction to my grip on him.

He filled me. The pressure he applied to my walls was a mix of pain and pleasure.

He was too much for me. I knew that the day we went swimming in the waterfall pool in the rainforest. I knew I'd never had his kind of big before and that enticed me.

I gritted my teeth, forcing myself to adjust, mindful of not making a single noise because I didn't want to disrupt how lost he'd gotten in me.

I was worried.

Worried that if he came to his senses, this would all just stop.

His head remained slung back as he pumped forth, maintaining his firm grip on my hips. And I let him stay that way. Because Yusuf looked like what we were doing had him caught up in a trance. In an escape. Grunting and groaning softly with his eyes closed. Rocking into me with ease and squeezing my hips whenever my walls reacted to the friction he created between us.

I tried biting my lips closed to keep any sounds to myself.

Why I would put myself through such torture made little sense to me. But seeing him like this, in his own world, focus fixed on whatever feeling he was journeying through. It was lubricating what was happening between us. Making my toes curl, even though soft and slow, wasn't my thing in the least.

Yusuf sliding in and out felt good, though. His reach against my spot was increasing sensitivity gradually. So much so, when I exhaled, I moaned.

And that broke him out of whatever or *wherever* he was.

Yusuf immediately stopped.

Paused in place.

Shit!

He leveled his head again, eyes landing on me. Both of our chests were rising and falling with our breaths. Sweat had gathered along the hairs on his brows and on the space just below his neck, which I could see beneath the unbuttoned top of his Hawaiian shirt.

His grip around my hips loosened, and he moved a hand off my hip to grab the back of my head to lift me out of my incline, bringing me closer to him so he could kiss me. Instead of a crash of our lips, it was a soft landing. He kissed me for a few breaths, both of us panting our way through it. He hadn't resumed though, and inside I was longing and panicking.

"Do you have any triggers?" he asked against my lips.

Asked it so gently I thought I had misheard him.

"What?"

"Triggers." His lips were off mine and making its way to my neck where he left soft kisses and a warm breath along the most sensitive parts. My neck was my most sensitive erogenous zone. His kisses distracted me, so there was no way his question was getting answered properly.

I moaned. "I don't understand the question."

"What do you like done…?" He dragged his tongue up my skin and my walls tightened around him, which made him groan. "… in bed?"

"Right about now you can do whatever you want to me."

He chuckled, then moaned. "That might be biting off more than you can chew."

My eyes popped open with that. Anticipation made me wetter between us.

"I usually take my time," he continued against my skin. "Learn what you like. At least that's what I did with—"

"Yusuf." I leaned away for only a second to add that, "I'm a simple woman. I have uncomplicated likes that don't need learning or studying. Just fuck me, okay? Really hard and very good."

He arched a brow.

"I like it hard." I nodded. "See? Simple."

"Cool." He smirked. Yusuf repositioned the nook of my right knee to rest on his forearm and he slid me forward and added, "I like it hard and very good, too."

His movements were way more concise than before to prove that. And unrelenting. It's like he found his rhythm, found my spot, and put his strokes on cruise control until I could barely keep my eyes on his.

We made a chorus of moans and groans between us. Every inch of him pushing and sliding between my slick walls was causing a fire I wanted to burn me from the inside out.

And it did. Because he had a hand on my neck, his tongue down my throat, and his dick so far deep in me and in places I never knew men could reach without their hands. There was nothing left for me to do but to come.

And I did.

Hard.

Losing all sense of time and place and even space. I could no longer feel the table's cool surface beneath me, couldn't hear the ocean's waves undulating anymore. I could barely hear myself breathing.

I wanted to announce I was coming. Just so he could keep doing whatever the hell he was doing to me, but I also didn't want to disrupt the momentum between us.

Plus, I'd have to have control of my mouth to voice a sentence and I couldn't do that either.

All I could do was feel myself unravel.

I had no control, and I wanted none back if that meant the sensation of pleasure running laps through me on repeat would meet its end. The moment was the longest few seconds I'd ever experienced.

Near the tail end of that ride, I opened my eyes to his to find his attention completely on me. Each time our torsos slammed against each other; the meeting of our wet bodies clapped between us. Yusuf's bodily muscles, all of them, flexed in time with his hard colliding with my soft.

He made it impossible to look away from him.

"Fuck, Clarke," he whispered, clenching his jaw, arms quivering as he dropped his head back for only a second before leveling his eyes to refocus on me.

I was in his arms a moment later on the bed a second after, with my ass up in the air and him behind me sliding in again.

Wet blots covered our clothes everywhere. Completely drenched with sweat since we removed not a single item before we started. And judging by how eager Yusuf was with getting back into play, he didn't plan to stop to disrobe and neither did I.

Because Yusuf was fucking me like he had no plans of letting up and the orgasm he was working on getting out of me had me drifting off to another body shaking, mental getaway once again.

twelve

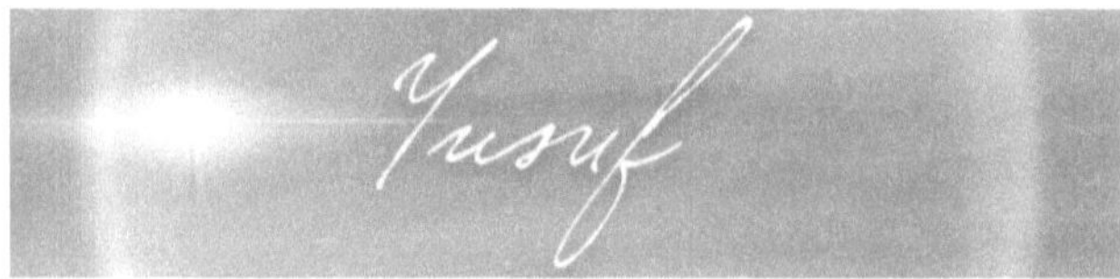

YUSUF

MORNING SUN RAYS rained down on me as I stood out on Clarke's patio sipping black coffee.

The ocean waves rose and fell on repeat in the distance, straight ahead of me. It was mesmerizing.

I closed my tired eyes, losing myself in the sweet, bitter caffeine.

A calm washed over me. A calm I haven't felt in too long.

I was dressed in only the white terrycloth robe, Clarke lent me, courtesy of the resort. I stood out on her patio attempting to get my bearings.

The woman had an appetite.

Her appetite was damn near insatiable.

And so was mine.

It was the first time in hours I had an opportunity to process everything that had happened in those last few hours. Which I could do because I was finally alone with my thoughts out on her patio, drinking coffee and catching my breath.

This experience, what happened between us the night before? What had been happening between us since then has been... surreal.

I was in Clarke's condo. Outside her bedroom on her patio with the knowledge of what she sounded like in ecstasy, what she tasted like coming, the way her deep stares wavered when at the very moment her body gave into her orgasm.

I'd met this woman only seven days ago.

Since the night before, we'd been having sex on and off for hours, both of us taking turns initiating whenever we couldn't take being around each other without being *on* one another.

There was familiarity between us at this point. She told me she wasn't someone to study, but for the past few hours, I have enjoyed exploring the depths of her body and all the things I could make it do with parts of mine.

I was on my last sip of coffee out on the patio when I felt her hands skating up my chest over the robe from behind.

We'd done this so much in the few hours that only her touch got me hard.

Because I knew it now. I'd learned what it meant and how to answer it.

She laid her head against my back and sent one of her hands down to my thigh, sliding her hand into the robe where it naturally divided, only stopping when she got my hard-on in her grip.

Clarke held me firm in her soft palm, twisting her wrist as she slid me in and out of her hand, and got me harder each time she stroked me back and forth.

She was very sexual. She enjoyed sex. The act anchored her in the now completely. At least with me. I've watched her lose herself in trembling sensations, fully deliver on being a vivid, endless fantasy. It was entertaining watching her work because you could tell she loved giving pleasure as much as she loved receiving it.

I'd left her in the bathroom after freshening up with brushing my teeth with a complementary toothbrush in her cabinet and showering in her shower.

Clarke had joined me in the shower, and we sexed there, making a mess of the soap and water on the tiled floor. Neither one of us came. Sex in the shower was just for fun. She was there and so was I. And it's like I said, for the last few hours we couldn't be around each other and not be on one another. So now Clarke was on the patio for the real thing.

I turned around to face her, moaning the second our eyes locked. She was fresh faced, no makeup. The outline of her lips was a little crimson from the kissing we've been doing nonstop. Her locs were up in a messy bun, appearing to be held there by nothing. I looked forward to messing that up.

I leaned to my left to place my ceramic mug on the patio's tiny glass table, feeling as she undid the belt that kept my robe cinched at my waist.

When I returned my attention to her, it was just as she was lowering down into a squat, right there out on the patio to guide me into her warm, wet mouth.

"*Mmm*, damn," I groaned, stumbling back a bit to adjust.

I slowly slung my head between my shoulders and reclined my lower back against the edge of the patio's railing.

The sun continued to pour down on me without a cloud to shield its rays. Warming me up in the terrycloth as Clarke warmed me up below.

They constructed the patio at a clever angle. It's like they knew to prepare for erotic moments like this. The people on her floor couldn't see what was happening. And we were too high up for people walking the grounds of the resort at that late morning hour to notice what we were doing. But the people in the building across from us could definitely get a show if they were out at that hour.

Which I didn't care about. I was too present. Biting my bottom lip and clutching the spools of locs in Clarke's bun to really care about anything else. All I could focus on doing was coming.

She moved at a rhythm, keeping her jaw firm. Causing so much slip she was slurping and gagging softly on me.

Clarke would look up at me every so often to catch my expressions, and I had plenty to give. So many to sort through.

I was close. Her tongue twisting and twirling around the head of my dick was making my knees weak. I wanted to guide her off, attempted to do just that when she grabbed me on either side of my hips to hold the terrycloth fabric tight in her grip.

"Shit, Clarke," I whispered, and groaned, returning to fisting her bun but now meeting her mouth with targeted thrusts forward.

"You want it?" I panted between breaths.

She nodded.

And that's all it took for me to give in.

Uncontrollable contractions of my muscles at the base of my dick fluttered like crazy. And she kept sucking and moaning as I came and the whole thing brought me to my toes, grunting and thrusting, aiming for her throat, unable to do anything else.

I reached down and took her in my arms soon after, and carried her to her bed through the patio's opened door. Placed her on her mattress at the same time as I grabbed the box of condoms she gave me earlier. There were only two condoms left and while that was disappointing, I had no time to stay in that feeling.

No refractory period needed between coming and sliding back into Clarke.

I loved the sensitivity, the slight bite of pain of reentering into her heat without giving my dick an opportunity to recover from its nut.

She was face down, ass high in the air with me behind her, watching her ass ripple from the collision of me sexing her from behind.

I took breaths through my teeth, listened to her muffled moans play around us like a ballad. And Clarke sang well like this. Far from the quiet type. If it felt good, she was loud. Really good... she was deafening.

I moved in close and wrapped an arm around her waist, aiming my fingers for her clit. And she made room for me. Spreading her thighs wider on her knees, then tossing a look over her shoulder when I circled the pads of my fingertips around her tiny ball while increasing my speed behind her.

"*Mmm*, Yusuf," she moaned, throwing herself back against me more. "Damn, you make me feel so good."

That brief look made me want to see her entirely. Clarke was too fine to fuck from behind for too long, anyway. I needed us face-to-face.

So that's what I did.

I turned her over, so she was on her back now with me on top of her.

We moaned together, gazing into each other's eyes. Her legs held back by my forearms, giving me the perfect angle against her spot. I felt the soft muscle contract and her walls trying to suck me in as the friction I caused between us made it hot down there.

"You're the best thing on this island," she remarked. Her eyelids gradually closed as her neck arched off her pillow while her hands fisted the sheets beneath us.

She was coming. The vision of her eyes rolling closed, her sweet voice being reduced to a whimper, while her pussy contracted and released me was all so intense, I had to let it all go too.

I leaned in close against her neck and whispered, "You are to me, too," filling the condom and collapsing on top of her soon after.

thirteen

CLARKE

"FRIEND, I have been surviving off of dick and orgasms for the past twenty-one hours and I love that for me," I said with a full mouth. "I think this is heaven, Esme."

Esme laughed on the other end of my phone. "You are chewing so loud in my ear."

"I'm starving!" I placed my hand beneath my mouth to catch the food threatening to fall out as I spoke. "I haven't eaten in hours."

"Damn!" She giggled. "Was it really like *that*?"

I stopped forking white coconut rice and teriyaki salmon into my mouth to close my eyes and press my hand to my chest.

"Yes." I nodded. "I haven't eaten since last night. It's almost five in the evening the next day here. The only reason he and I stopped, and he left to return to his room, is because we ran out of condoms. I am blissfully sore."

"Wow!"

"So, yes," I said, chewing. "It was really like *that*."

"I love that for you too, then."

I chuckled. "I usually can get in a couple of rounds, you know, keep going until I get mine. But I couldn't get enough of him. There was just something between us that was so insatiable, something so raw, fueling us both. I mean, how else would you explain having the energy to keep up without stopping to eat anything?"

"Well, damn." Esme sighed. "You're on a tropical island having great sex; Juliette's in Vegas, gambling and presumably having great sex and I'm... stuck in hot ass New York City, celibate - not by choice - and tutoring an elite prep school brat."

"Oh goodness, has he gotten worse?"

"He is the fucking worse." She grunted. "You know... when I took this damn tutoring job, I did so because it was paying better than what I earned during the school year, and I figured I could make some extra money on the side while school is out."

"I know."

"I didn't take it to be disrespected by a damn tween. I want to beat his little ass after every online session we have!"

I held my hand to my mouth to laugh while chewing. My girl Esme was the calmest and most patient out of our trio. Nothing much upset her or had the power to get her this way. So if she was fuming over a child, the problem was definitely that child.

"And I don't get it. I don't know what happened," she continued. "We got along wonderfully during the first three weeks of summer tutoring, but then, just like that..." She snapped her fingers. "He switched up on me. The only saving grace, the *only* reason I'm sincerely tolerating this kid during summer break, is his dad. He's so sweet and excels at explaining away his son's terrible behavior so empathetically. It's attractive. Endearing. And when he does it, it makes me question if I hallucinated that child's bullshit. But... I can't help but to look forward to our weekly video calls discussing his son's progress."

I smiled. "'Cause he's fine, huh?"

"Rich *and* fine," she commented. "And you know that's my catnip."

We shared a laugh at that.

"It's exactly how I like them to be."

"Oh, I know that well."

"Anyway," she started again, inhaling and exhaling deeply. "Let's talk no more about that. I'm feeling my pressure climb, reliving shit on the weekend. Let me at least enjoy that, right?"

"How many more weeks do you have with him?"

"Four," she answered. "And week four can't get here fast enough. When do you return to New York?"

"The Sunday after next."

"*Oooh*," she crooned. "So, you get more than enough time with your island boo."

I snickered and blushed. Did not know I could do both at the same time. But it didn't surprise me I could when the topic was Yusuf. Just thinking about him was getting me hot again.

"So, like, do you think something will come of all this?" Esme quizzed.

I shook my head. "I'm not thinking about that." I forked more food into my mouth. "We are having fun. For once, I'm not marrying men in my head and thinking further than the moment."

"Understood."

"He still has this unbreakable bond to his wife from her grave. It's admirable and a little self-defeating, but I'm cool with this just being what it is - hot ass sex on a beautiful island that we'll both leave separately in a little over a week. I'm here for a good time. That's it. I refuse to trip off how temporary this is."

* * *

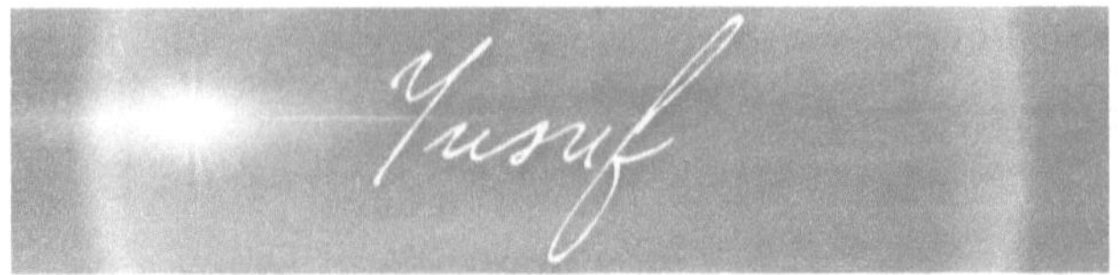

YUSUF

"I'm trippin'," I mumbled to myself.

I placed the container with the rest of my food onto the coffee table and leaned back in my seat on the couch. I was in the living room... and sitting across from my wife's urn.

I moved the urn from my bedroom a few days ago and hadn't taken it back. When I returned from Clarke's condo earlier that evening, the purple and gold vase was there to greet me as I walked through my front door.

I felt like a teenager who'd spent the night out, way past curfew, doing ratchet shit with his ratchet friends, and didn't call his parents, and now it was time to face the music. Because they were there, in the living room, in front of the couch, calling his ass to have a seat in front of them to be questioned.

And to anyone else, I'm sure they would see just an urn. A beautifully constructed rounded vase that looked more like home decor and less like the source of the guilt building in me the longer I looked at it, but to me, it was a representation of my wife Parris.

I swallowed the last of my food and used the tip of my tongue to clean around my gums.

I replayed Clarke and my time together, on and on, after leaving her room. We'd had sex until room service delivered our food from one of the resort's restaurants. I left soon after because we'd run out of condoms after that.

I didn't want to leave. I wanted to stay there for more.

She and I got the same welcome bag from our solo travelers group and I had condoms in mine, too. Thought to let Clarke know that after I ate my food in my room... but then I returned to my room and saw the urn.

The urn was my entire reason for being here on this island.

To scatter Parris's ashes.

She had A Last Will and Testament created after her brain aneurysm two years ago. Decided to put in her Will, she wanted to be cremated, which I was totally against. I was against a lot of the discussions about death, to be honest. Very uncooperative in some regard, although I showed support with everything else. I loved my wife. In every sense of the word, I loved her and when I said we'd be together forever; I meant forever with my entire being. So, the thought of her dying, the talks about what would happen if she *were* to die, I exited them all. I wanted nothing to do with them. Yet, she asked in her Will to have her remains scattered on the shoreline at Makena State Park Little Beach, where we first said I love you, on the birthday after her death at sunrise.

Last year she passed away shortly before her birthday, four months before, and I couldn't bring myself to let her go. My therapist labeled my hesitation attachment issues that stemmed from my atypical grieving. I call it loving my wife with everything in me.

Although I didn't agree with her being cremated, having her remains made me feel like I still had *her*. To me, the urn was still her. I spoke to it daily, addressed it whenever I entered any room it was in. It was her to me.

So, seeing it after returning from Clarke's condo after our hours long of sex had me trippin'.

I ran a hand down my mouth and leaned forward, dropping my head to my chest.

"I'm sorry," I apologized low. "You sent me here to do something, and I fucked up."

I glanced out of my patio at my mountain view, then looked back at the urn.

"It's just... I didn't want to come here." I pointed at her urn. "And you knew that. You had to know I wouldn't want to come here to scatter your ashes, Parris."

I shut my eyes, squeezing my lids shut, shaking my head.

"This has been really hard, baby," I confessed. "Really, really hard. You know I have never cheated on you. Never had a want to. I knew there were beautiful women all over this world, but I knew beauty faded. And what we had, what we cultivated between us, was everlasting and was superior to all that other superficial shit."

I ran my hand down my close shaved head, then over my face.

"She is *not* you. Clarke can never, *ever* be you. Because she's Clarke. And Clarke is *so* fucking incredible. My God, she's amazing, Parris. And... she has made me feel more like *me* again, you know? I've been in therapy since your death, have been seeing a doctor for a little over a year and he hasn't been able to make me feel what Clarke has made me feel in seven days and I'm not talking about the sex. How the hell is that possible?"

My eyes locked on the structure of the urn. The weight of my heart feeling heavier in my chest forced me to look away.

"And one part of me feels like shit for all the things I've let happen between Clarke and I since arriving on this island because the only reason I'm here is because you sent me here and you sent me here to scatter your ashes on the island we first said I love you to each other on. But then." I licked my lips. "The other part of me wants to get lost in her again. To forget *why* I'm here, to shed the only thing of you I have left. The other part of me wants to make a new reason to be here and not teeter on the edge of depression. To numb the sadness, I feel down in my bones, that I feel at only the idea of having nothing left of you ever again after next week."

I took a breath to hold back the tears pooling in my eyes.

"For those first few minutes? When she and I were having sex? I thought of you." I nodded slowly. "I closed my eyes the moment I slid inside her and pictured you. Because I still can remember how you looked and what you felt like when we made love, baby. And for those first few minutes, she *was* you and it was a little like coming home to you after wanting to come home but being unable to for over a year."

But then Clarke moaned, and her moan pulled me out of that moment and back into Clarke's carefreeness. Because Clarke was *not* Parris.

And that realization led me to remember Parris wasn't there. And Parris not being there was why I'd been so sad, why I'd been so fucked up over her being gone for over a year. I needed to escape that thought again, to run from those feelings. To replace the heartache of it all. I needed a distraction and Clarke had been an excellent one since the flight to Hawaii.

I liked that.

I liked her.

And standing there between her legs, inside her warmth, she felt as good as she looked.

So, we had sex. Really *great* sex that ended, then started again until it was ending and starting more than I could keep count. And I thought nothing of it, didn't let myself think of nothing else besides fucking her. Didn't have enough time to myself to think of anything else, anyway. Because we had the backdrop of Hawaii serving as an aphrodisiac and pure attraction running through our veins. It was destined to happen.

But now I was back in my condo, sitting across from my wife, feeling like shit because my wife sent me to this island, an island we first said we loved each other on, to scatter her ashes... but I came here and fucked another woman.

And... I wouldn't want Parris to do the same if I were the one who died.

... because I'm a hypocrite.

I squeezed my lids closed and dropped my head to pinch the bridge of my nose.

"I'm so sorry, baby," I whispered.

Sorry, because of what I did... and sorry that, if given the opportunity, I would definitely do it again.

fourteen

CLARKE

"AND WHAT WILL YOU HAVE TONIGHT?"

I smiled up at the Hawaiian server and answered, "I'll have a Mai Tai and the fish basil over tropical pineapple fried rice."

I occupied a seat in one of the resort's Hawaiian-Thai fusion restaurants across from Yusuf. When he called my room to invite me out to dinner, I was lowkey excited. And I was lowkey, wondering if he would reach out to me after our hookup, so that definitely added to my excitement.

I shifted my focus on him as the server collected our menus to leave. He smiled at me and I couldn't help but to return a smile back.

I'll admit, I agreed to accompany him to dinner to feed my curiosity. I wanted to know how things would be between us, post-hookup.

Would it be awkward or weird?

Would we be able to look each other in the eye?

I had parts of Yusuf inside and out of me. I honestly never wanted to get any of him off me. Tasting him was the greatest turn on. Watching him come almost brought me to the point of coming myself.

When he left my room, he seemed fine, but a lot can change when you're alone with your thoughts.

"You look beautiful tonight," he complimented, then shrugged a shoulder. "Then again. You always look beautiful."

I blushed. "And you look handsome, as always."

Yusuf licked his lips really slowly, and I had to look away, as if doing so could hide how smitten this man had me.

"So..." I cleared my throat and crossed my legs under our table. "About the other night... *and* day."

He chuckled. "You always want to discuss these things."

"I always want to be on the same page," I corrected. "Yes, I do."

He nodded his agreement. "Touché. Okay." Yusuf scooted to the edge of his seat. "What happened between us was a great escape for me and I hope it was for you, too."

"My sentiments are the same."

"Good." He nodded slowly.

Yusuf smirked knowingly then winked when I refused to break eye contact first.

"Oh my God." I smiled shyly. "Will you quit making me blush?"

He shook his head from side to side. "No."

I tossed my head back in a laugh.

When I leveled my head to lock eyes with him again, one of the other patrons caught my eye instead. It wasn't really them. It's what they held in their grip.

"Oh!" I tilted my head to one side. "They serve wine here?"

"Yup."

"I didn't see it on the drink menu."

"There's a separate one with the wines listed. You like to drink wine?"

"Do I *like* to drink wine?" I scoffed a laugh. "Wine is my love language."

"You're a fan."

"More like a stan. If I could travel the world wine tasting everywhere I went, I'd die a thrilled woman." I gasped, slapping my hand to my mouth. "I'm so sorry."

He chuckled. "What I tell you about apologizing to me?"

I smiled.

"I never understood wine," he admitted next. "They all taste the same to me."

"You people drive me nuts when you all say *that*. Not all wine *tastes* the same. Like, at all."

"Heard it all before, huh?"

"Too many times." I giggled. "My grandmother is a retired sommelier, so maybe that's why I understand wine completely."

"A sommelier." He did a shrugging motion with the corners of his mouth. "Fancy."

"Oh, Nana's the belle of the ball."

He snickered.

"She taught me everything there is to know about wine. From oak barrels to the quality of aging processes." I giggled lowly. "Before she fell ill, she managed our family winery out in Napa Valley."

His brows shot up. "You're the heir to a winery."

"Was," I corrected. "She sold it. With no one else in the family willing to run and manage everything, she sold it five years ago, which was, interestingly, the year I realized law may not be for me. I *loved* that winery." I kissed my teeth. "If I realized sooner, I didn't want to practice law, I would've snatched it up. We still own our oak barrel business. My father manages it. He sees more value in that business than the business of running a winery."

"That's really amazing, Clarke." He held up a finger. "Not your dad not valuing the winery, but you. You have a history that is amazing."

We held a stare for a moment before I broke mine to look down at my hands.

I wanted him so badly.

"School me."

I looked up at him again. "What?"

"Give me a crash course on how to drink wine." He shrugged. "I don't know. Teach me what you know. I want to experience wine the way you do because I swear to you, whenever I drink it, I just taste... wine."

I cringed. "*Please* stop saying that."

He laughed.

"Then teach me." Yusuf rested his broad shoulders against the back of his seat and chucked his chin. "I'm an excellent student, as you've learned, I hope."

A chill ran down my back at that, making me shiver. I ran my palm along the back of my neck in my attempt to calm down.

"Where do we start?"

"Uh..." I shook my head to recover. "I guess we can get the cheapest bottle of wine and one that costs a little more and compare and contrast?"

Yusuf's hand went up a second later, and our server was at our table less than a minute after.

"Can you bring us a bottle of your least expensive wine and another bottle of your most expensive bottle of wine—"

"Wait, no." I perked up. "Not *most* expensive. Just a little more expensive—"

"No limitations," he cut in again. "If we're going to do this, I want to really do it." His focus shifted to the server again. "Least expensive bottle and most expensive bottle, please."

I opened my mouth with intentions to contest his request but asked the server, "Can I view your wine menu?"

She was kind enough to hand one to me from a neighboring table.

"The most expensive wine is $300," I informed Yusuf.

He lifted his glass to his lips to sip, then asked nonchalantly, "Do you recognize the brand's name?"

Not even a flinch at the mention of the bottle's price.

"*Umm...*" I cleared my throat, trying like hell not to show how very turned on he was making me by just being him. "No."

"Cool." He rubbed his hands together. "I'm excited."

We didn't have to wait long for our wine. Someone other than our server brought it to our table. A black man, who wore a white linen shirt with a lei around his neck.

A sommelier.

I smiled with delight when he held each bottle, one at a time, with the neck laying on the inside of his forearm, displaying the label to Yusuf and I. In front of us, he uncorked the two bottles of wine and placed the corks from each bottle in front of us.

Yusuf glanced down at it, confused.

"He wants us to see that the wine isn't drenching the cork. Lightly stained is good. Drenched in wine is bad."

"Ah, I see," Yusuf replied. "So these are good."

"These are great," I whispered in awe.

Our sommelier chuckled. "Connoisseur?"

I sputtered a laugh. "More like a *wannabe* sommelier."

With our wine freshly uncorked and four glasses on our table, thanks to us informing the sommelier we were conducting an experiment and needed over two wine glasses, I poured out the wine from the cheapest bottle.

Yusuf reached for the glass, and I laid a hand on top of his to stop him.

"Don't be so quick to sip it," I told him softly. "I have to give you instructions first."

He threw his hands up. "Oh, of course, my apologies. Where are my manners?"

I smirked in response.

"To really taste both wines," I started. "We have to send the wine to the back of our tongues, and slowly roll it around our mouths in a swishing motion, but not like we're gargling mouthwash, which you could do but don't."

"Noted."

"We're looking for the subtleties. The flavors. Ready?"

He nodded, bringing the glass to his lips to take a sip.

I smelled the wine in the glass first and shrugged, unimpressed. From the color staining my glass, I could tell the taste of the wine wouldn't be anywhere near expressive. I tilted the glass in front of my lips, anyway, sending the wine to the back of my tongue. I rolled it around my mouth, searching, then swallowed.

"Okay," I started. "It isn't bad, right?"

"Not to me."

"I could tell from the color it didn't age in a barrel for long. This batch likely did most of its aging in this bottle. And when it was in a barrel, the barrel was a neutral barrel and not new oak."

"Why does that matter?" He asked. "Why does barrel matter?"

I beamed. "The barrel is the holy grail of taste. Next is vineyard location, and when they harvested the grapes.

I swirled the wine around the glass and gave it another sip.

"The barrel imparts tannins in wine. Tannins give the wine its taste. Certain elements in the type of oak used to make the barrels end up in the wine. Oak barrels impart flavors like vanilla, smoke, wood, and spice when they age wine in them. Sometimes you can even taste manure—"

"Shit?"

I cackled. "Yes, okay, fine, yes. Shit... *used* to keep the acres of land fertile for growing. The grape takes on the flavors of the land it grows on. That's why every wine has its own unique taste."

He snickered, raising the glass to his lips again to sip. "I don't taste any of that in this. The flavors? Nothing." He shook his head. "I just taste... wine."

"Because they probably aged this wine in a neutral barrel," I reasoned. "After extended use, oak barrels no longer impart flavor, but..." I held up a finger. "Neutral barrels can still serve as aging vessels. That's why this wine still has the base elements to taste and look like wine, but also why this wine is inexpensive."

I placed my glass on the table and picked up the least expensive bottle of wine we ordered. "The more expensive the bottle of wine, the more details you're going to get." I pointed at the label. "This label only tells us the year they harvested the grape, which was 2018, a good year for wine, by the way." I winked.

He smiled.

"It's made from Cabernet Sauvignon, grown in California. Which is typical. Cabernet Sauvignon does well in California because of that state's weather and climate. But that's all we know about this wine. The grapes grew, and the makers of *this* wine harvested them in California. But what part of California? On how many acres of land? The grapes used to make this wine could have been harvested from several vineyards all over California, then combined and poured into this one bottle, for all we know. Details matter if you're looking for taste. The more expensive the bottle of wine, the more details you're going to get about it on the label."

"So, the label sets the price of the wine."

"No." I shook my head. "There are other factors. Region, vineyard, type of aging process, whether it's barrel or bottle, reputation, and marketing, of course. But the thing that sets the price is the region. And while Cali is the perfect state, the city is what's the winner."

"What city is the best to grow grapes for wine?"

"Napa." I smiled big. "My grandmother's vineyard, or what *was* her vineyard, is in Napa."

"Interesting," he exclaimed. "All of this is..."

"Fascinating."

"*A lot* is what I was going for."

I laughed. "It's *everything* to me! Now back to label."

"Yes, of course, professor." He gestured. "Please continue."

"Case in point." I giggled, picking up the expensive bottle of wine and immediately swooning at the info. "*This* label is giving us *all* the deets."

He focused on the printed wording.

"It tells us that not only were the grapes grown and harvested in California, also in 2018 like our cheaper wine, but that the grapes were grown in the world-renowned Napa Valley of Cali. They even tell us the number of acres they harvested the grapes from. See?"

"Wow, yeah," he acknowledged lowly. "Damn."

"I know, right?" I turned the bottle to view the label again. "I can already tell we're in for a treat."

I poured out a little of the wine into another two clean wine glasses for us to try.

And when I took my first sip, I closed my eyes and moaned. A rush of memories took over, sending me through a handful of emotions until I finally opened my eyes to him.

"Okay." I scooted my way to the edge of my seat. "If you tell me this just tastes like wine to you, I will scream."

He smiled widely. "Then... I *won't* say it."

I released a loud laugh.

"Yusuf! You don't taste that?"

Yusuf took another swig and rolled it around on his tongue for a few seconds.

"This one is *so* rich." I lifted my glass to sip it again, and it was better than the first time. "Whereas with the other one, the woody taste was subtle, which means their wine spent less time in the barrel. But *this* bad ass? Whew!" I giggled. "The makers of this wine aged her like the fine wine she is. I'm getting every bit of the barrel she grew up in. The cedar, the vanilla. This brand definitely ages their wines in brand new French oak barrels *every time*. At least they did with this bottle."

He looked at me wide eyed. "And you got all of that from one sip?"

"Along with the memories," I whispered. "Yes."

Yusuf tilted his head to his left. "Explain that to me."

"Gladly." I beamed with delight. "Okay, you know how certain songs and scents remind you of places and people?"

He nodded. "Yeah. I know that well."

I nodded too. "Wine does that for me." I licked my lips, wanting to savor the remnants of wine on my lips. "I taste leather."

He blinked hard. "Leather?"

"Yeah." I chuckled. "It's weird, I know, but it's there. It reminds me of my late grandfather. He passed when I was away on a girls' trip with my friends five years ago. One of my most favorite people. He *loved* leather. Wore it year-round. Leather pants, leather coats, leather boots, leather shorts, and his coveted leather vests." I smiled, the tears pooling in my eyes. "He *always* smelled like leather."

Yusuf stared at me for a short while, then said, "You love wine."

I blinked back my tears and sat up in my seat.

"People always say they love wine, but you?" He pointed. "You *really* love wine."

"I *really* do," I replied, finishing the rest of the wine in my glass.

"And... if you want to be a sommelier," he added, "find out what you need to do to become that."

"I know what to do. It's just—"

Our server returned to our table with another server, placing our plates of food in front of Yusuf and me.

"It's just, what?" Yusuf asked as soon as we were alone again.

"It's too late." I shrugged, forking some of the fish into my mouth and chewing a bit before continuing. "I went to school to study law. I wanted to be a lawyer. But I keep failing the bar, so I'm stuck working as a paralegal, which I really am hating, but... I made my choice."

"Then make another one. You know you can change your mind, right, Clarke?" Yusuf scooted forward. "I was in school for computer engineering. Hated my university's curriculum my first semester and almost fell into a depression in my second year when I started taking computer engineering intro courses. So, I dropped out soon after Parris and I got married. My mother was livid. My decision confused Parris, but I did it anyway and never looked back. Photography was my passion. Photography has *always* been my passion, and I pursued it full throttle after dropping out. We struggled for a little, but fuck it. I decided I would rather struggle while going after my passion than struggle to live a life I absolutely hated. And I maintained that until things eventually changed. Money trickled in until it started to downpour from everywhere. Eventually, I was creating jobs out of thin air and making money from them. A company paid Parris and I 1.3 million to sponsor a series of videos using their products, the biggest check we'd ever gotten, that *I'd* ever gotten in my life."

"Wow," I exhaled. "That's... incredible."

"*You're* incredible and you *love* wine." He jabbed the table with his fingertip. "It's clearly your passion. You light up in a way I've never seen a person light up when talking about wine. Quit being a wannabe sommelier and go for yours."

"You sure you don't also moonlight as a motivational speaker on top of everything else?"

He chuckled, forking a little food into his mouth. I did the same.

"I'm getting you another bottle of that expensive wine for you to have by yourself."

I popped my head up from my plate. "Oh, no, Yusuf." I pressed a hand to my chest. "You don't have to."

"I want to."

We locked eyes when he took my hand in his.

"And... when we're done..." He smiled. "I'd like to show you the mountain view, if that's okay."

I blinked repeatedly. "Oh?"

"You showed me *your* ocean view." He smirked. "It's only fair I show you, *my* mountain view."

I snickered.

"Sound good?"

I smiled. Well, really, I melted into the wicker seat at both the thought of having more of the expensive wine and getting more time with Yusuf alone.

"Yes." I nodded. "That sounds great."

* * *

We were on each other by the time we reached the threshold of Yusuf's condo.

He and I kept it together long enough to finish dinner, our bottle of wine - the expensive bottle, of course - and for Yusuf to cover the check.

I tried to tell him I'd pay for my portion of the bill, but he refused for me to even finish suggesting we go Dutch. It annoyed him, actually.

That was refreshing.

With the new corked bottle of that $300 wine, we tried at the restaurant in his grasp, I pulled Yusuf to me when we arrived in front of his door and kissed him.

He got the door unlocked, like he did with my condo the night we first hooked up, and we were in his condo soon after.

His condo was like mine. Same kitchen to greet us at the door. An unobstructed view of the patio. Only difference was his view was of the mountains. Moss covered the tops of peaks like caps of snow, only green. It was nighttime now, so the sky was blue black with specs of silver sparkling here and there along the sky.

It was beautiful, but I only glimpsed all that because all I could see kissing Yusuf was him.

He moaned against me, his free hand holding me close to his chest. Broke our kiss momentarily to leave the wine bottle on the kitchen counter before he took me into his arms again.

We'd arrived in the living room where he balanced me on the console table beneath his flatscreen. His hands moved all over me, cupping my breasts, brushing warm hands down my neck, before his lips followed the trail his hands created.

He kissed me from my lips to my cheek, my cheek to my neck. And I relished in it all, closing my eyes and dropping my head back between my shoulders.

I'd only leveled my head for a moment and opened my eyes for half a second when I glimpsed the purple jar with gold trimming sitting on his coffee table.

"That's beautiful," I whispered, then moaned, cupping the back of his head with my palm.

He pulled me to the edge of the console table and closer to him, using the sides of my thighs, and whispered back, "What's beautiful?"

"That jar on your coffee table." I bit my bottom lip as I glided my hand down his shorts' crotch to palm his bulge. "I don't have any decor in my room besides the ocean-themed paintings on the walls."

"I don't have a jar," he revealed nonchalantly.

That made my eyes pop open. I glanced over his shoulder again, to be sure. Squinted my eyes at the tiny jar next.

"Of course, you do." I said with a giggle. "That purple gold thing over there."

He froze against me.

When he leaned back a bit, we locked eyes, and his expression made me knit my brows.

I couldn't place my finger on the look at first, couldn't quite read the clenching of his jaw and his blank stare on the wall behind me or his need to suddenly create space between us.

"What is it?" I asked. "What's wrong?"

"That's... *not* a jar." He pointed his thumb over his shoulder at it. "It's an urn."

"An urn?" I bounced my eyes from him to the urn, then back to him. "What an odd decor item."

"Shit... *umm*... damn." Yusuf created even more space between us while pinching the inner corners of his eyes with his finger tips. "It isn't a decor item, Clarke." His eyes were on mine again when he added, "It's my wife."

I couldn't have heard that clearly.

I shook my head once, confused at first, but I was smart enough to put two and two together.

An urn. His wife.

Duh, right?

But still I asked, "What do you mean it's your wife, Yusuf?"

Yusuf took a deep breath in and puffed his cheeks as he blew his exhale through his lips.

I pointed at the urn. "Are you... are you trying to tell me *your wife* is inside of that thing? Is *that* what you're telling me right now?"

"Yes." He swallowed hard. "That is what I am telling you."

And that snatched me completely out of the mood because...

"What the fuck?"

Yusuf held up both hands in front of him. "I can explain."

"Okay." I nodded, gesturing for him to do as promised. "Please do?"

"The urn," he started. "I brought the urn with me to scatter my wife's ashes."

"Why would you..." I glanced at it again. "Why would you bring your wife's urn to scatter her ashes while you're on vacation?"

"I didn't come to Maui on vacation."

My lips were in position to question that until the memory took over. He's been so cryptic about being back in Maui but not transparent about his motivation to fly here.

I squeezed my eyes closed, then pressed my fingers to my lids. When I opened them again, I asked, "*Why* are you in Maui Yusuf?"

He stared at me.

"Did you come back here only to scatter her ashes?"

"Yes," he answered, not missing a beat. "My only reason for returning to Maui was to scatter her ashes."

I covered my mouth with my hand.

"I didn't want to come back here," he admitted, shaking his head. "I never wanted to come back here, not without her. But... she put it in her Will. She wanted to be cremated and she wanted her ashes scattered in Maui, at sunrise, on Makena State Park Little Beach, on the first birthday after her death—"

"Oh, my God," I stage whispered.

"But." He ran his hands down his face. "I... I couldn't bring myself to let her go last year when her birthday arrived four months after she passed."

"Oh. My. God." The more I heard, the worse I felt.

It was selfish, I know, but all I could think was why me, *again*? Why couldn't I just meet a guy, like him, he like me, and we start something without impeding on something else? You know, like normal people?

Why did it always have to be the same story, just different male characters with my love life?

Fuck!

"My grief support group, my therapist, Parris's mother... they all encouraged me to go through with meeting Parris's last wishes for her birthday this year which is next Saturday. They told me I would feel better, but I just couldn't do it alone. So, I joined the Island Hop solo travelers' group earlier this year when there were only a few spots left. I needed the distraction. I needed not to feel alone on this island."

"I have to go," I announced, hopping down off the console table. "I can't—"

"Clarke—"

"It's fine." I shook my head. "I mean... it's *not* fine, but I just can't with this." I gestured at the urn, then pressed my hand to my chest. "I'm like... the other woman yet again."

"No, Clarke." He shook his head. "You're not."

"Yes." I nodded. "I *am*. You are here because of your wife. Your reason is your wife. You traveled all this way to do this thing, and I knew you still loved your wife. I knew there was some sense of loyalty to her you wanted to maintain and every chance I got, I've influenced your decision to forget all that."

"I'm a grown ass man, Clarke," he told me sternly. "I can make my own decisions. I'm not influenced by anything but me being attracted to you." He approached. "But not just your looks, your energy. Your amazing energy. The way you make me feel whenever I'm around you, in the same place as you." Yusuf pressed his hand to his chest. "You've given me something that no one else has given me since my wife died. You've given me hope that life continues, and being sincerely happy can happen after grief. That there's sunlight after a very dark time. And I don't regret a single thing about what we've done in Maui, Clarke. I regret nothing we've done since we've met."

His words went right to my heart. Warmed it and made it skip beats. They were genuine, his words. Honest. And they sounded amazing coming out of his mouth.

But... that damn urn.

Sitting there, beautifully.

It was also loud as fuck. Its purpose for being here. That serendipity, I thought, was a reality between Yusuf and I, was actually a coincidence because he wasn't even here for any of it.

He was here for his wife.

The urn made things abundantly clearer that this thing between Yusuf and I was very temporary. I was feeling like I didn't want it to be. And although I told Esme I was only having fun, a part of me hoped it could be a little more than that.

No.

I was hoping it could be *a lot* more than that.

But that damn urn.

I shook my head. "This is just way beyond anything I can deal with right now, Yusuf. I'm sorry."

I met my eyes with his and immediately noticed the sadness in them.

But... I couldn't.

And I couldn't take the sight of seeing him that way either.

So, I left without saying goodbye.

Turning on my sandals and taking large steps toward his condo's front door, leaving him alone... with his wife.

* * *

YUSUF

I stood in front of her door for a few minutes, six to be exact, when I arrived on her floor.

Should've stayed my ass in my condo. Her leaving was probably for the best. But I couldn't stay away from *her*.

It's baffling.

I'd gone *years* without knowing Clarke. But in one week, the idea of not seeing her again was a daunting one.

I lifted my fist and used my knuckles to rap against the white core door a few times. Stepped back a bit and waited.

Revealing my intentions for being in Maui was something I'd planned to do. But there just never seemed to be a good time to do it.

I didn't know Clarke well enough when we first met to tell her my reason for traveling to Maui. And by the time the opportunity to do so presented itself, I didn't want for her reaction to be what she ended up having, anyway.

Clarke opened her door less than a minute later.

She stood at the threshold in a crimson university tee and a pair of silk pajama shorts. Her locs were up in a bun at the top of her head, held together by something I could never figure out what it was.

I held up the sealed $300 bottle of wine I bought for her at the

143

restaurant we dined in less than an hour prior. "You left this behind when you stormed out."

"Oh?" she commented. "Is this like... my glass slipper? Since everything else practically turned into a pumpkin tonight, I guess it's fitting."

"Clarke..."

She'd turned and walked away from the door.

I didn't wait for an invitation to walk in behind her, allowing the condo's door to shut behind me.

I placed the wine bottle on her kitchen counter at the same time Clarke turned to face me.

"You should go back to your condo," she told me.

"I'm sorry."

She dropped her hands to her sides and shook her head. "Don't apologize. You did nothing wrong, Yusuf."

"I kept something from you."

"It wasn't my place for you to tell me anything. You don't owe me, Yusuf. We're not... this thing between us isn't... it's just... I don't even know." She gave into the heaviness in her head, dropping her head back between her shoulders. "I don't even know what to feel right now."

Neither did I.

Maui wasn't even an island I wanted to return to. There were too many memories buried in every part of this place.

This was Parris and my getaway spot.

It was *our* spot.

I imagined us still traveling here when we were old and gray, barely able to take part in the snorkeling and waterskiing activities we loved indulging in when we were younger because our limbs were too frail to keep up. So, we'd lounge on the beach most of the time, reminiscing about the old times, reliving our memories together. I had visions of us in our senior years because, in my eyes, I never thought we wouldn't get there together.

Because I actually imagined growing old with my wife. I looked forward to it.

A heavy feeling I'd done well with avoiding since arriving in Maui gradually resurfaced. It ached for me in my heart and made my stomach weak. And I refused to feel that. Because I'd experienced joy again and it was way too sedating for me to allow myself to feel the pain.

I locked eyes with Clarke again. She looked so bothered, so conflicted, but above all that, in need. I recognized the want in her eyes but the hesitance, too.

The doubts and the desires. The *should we* and the *we really shouldn't*.

It was palpable between us. Submerging.

I'd wade through those feelings for her, though.

I approached her slowly, and she took one step back.

"Yusuf," she whispered, then swallowed hard. "You should go back to your condo."

My hand slipped between her arm and her ribs, and she moaned against me when I took her face in my other hand.

"After," I promised against her lips. "I'll go back after."

She gave in, letting her weight go in my arms, parting her lips with mine as our tongues met instantly.

Against the wall in her condo's corridor, we kissed wildly, pulling at each other's clothing, the ones covering our most sensitive parts of us at least.

Her nipple was in my mouth and my hand down her silk pajama shorts when the thought that I could still end this crossed my mind.

Clarke was so warm against me though, sounding so sweet in my ears, humming her moans. I stroked her clit and circled my tongue around the tight skin of her nipple at the same speed.

We should stop, continued to play on in my mind from the corridor to the couch, where I placed her on the cushion and buried my lips in her wetness. Her essence slicked my lips and coiled the hairs on my trimmed mustache and goatee. And she kept them covered with her slow gyrations against my tongue, watching me as I licked and sucked between her lower lips. She watched until her body was jerking back and forth, back arching off the couch, and her jaw dropping to let out a silent cry.

I should leave, was the wordless agreement between the two of us when I pulled my shirt off and stepped out of my shorts to sheathe my erection with the condom I retrieved from the box in my Island Hop welcome bag.

But neither of us wanted me to stop, because what we wanted was to get lost in each other, in this moment.

I did not know what would come after this.

And for the first time. I sincerely didn't give a fuck.

I was still on my knees when Clarke threw the coral and green throw pillows to the floor. Her head was against the back of the couch, my grip on the neck. She reached down between us and guided me inside her slowly, moaning at every inch.

It didn't take long for soft pumps to become rhythmic thrusts and for my vision to blur before I gave into my heavy lids to accept the feel-good feeling sex with Clarke often provided and to accept the situation for what it was.

An escape.

A wet, tight escape that hugged me like it wanted me there forever with a woman I wouldn't mind having that with.

But I couldn't do that again. I couldn't trust time anymore. Forever had an expiration date. I'd learned that the hard way. So instead of living in fear of that, I forgot all of it and lost myself.

Lost myself in the moans we exhaled together in a duet.

Got lost in Clarke's insistence that we change positions for her to get on top.

She circled her hips to a rhythm only she could hear, but that we both enjoyed. I hung on to her cheeks as she lifted and dropped herself up and down on my lap. The sound of our bodies meeting ricocheting off the walls in competition with our grunts and growls.

She made the most beautiful face when she collided with bliss.

Brows bunched up a little over closed eyes. Head rolling around her neck until she let her head hang back as she surrendered to a release that had her walls contracting and releasing as I continued sliding in and out between them with well-timed upstrokes.

I was close too, so I quickly stood with her, placing her on the couch against the seat cushions but face down because I didn't want her to see me do it.

My intentions weren't to hide I was coming. I'd love for her to watch me do that.

I didn't want her to see me break.

Because I felt the urge to cry overwhelm me when the soles of my feet warmed beneath me.

The urge radiated from my heart, held me tight at my neck. I tried to swallow back what the urge created, but shit, everyone knows when you try not to cry, doing so only makes you cry harder. So, I forced myself to breathe through the feeling. But that didn't stop the tears from pricking the corners of my eyes.

The twitching at the base of my dick graduated to fluttering and soon the sensation arrested my mind with the need to come. And I allowed coming to take over, hoping it would stop the tears, but it didn't.

Coming only made me want to cry out more.

I moaned and groaned, thrusting in and out of her wet heat. Body shaking, heart racing, tears streaming down my eyes. And I went with the feeling. Whatever mixed bag of emotions and sensations that were running through me with fierce energy. A battle between my heart and my body conflicting with my soul.

Because although Clarke wasn't Parris, she was Clarke, and Clarke was an amazing woman too. In the short time of knowing her, I'd quickly grown to like her a lot... and realized in that instance I could probably love her too.

And that realization was no good for either of us.

fifteen

CLARKE

MY BODY WAS HURTING SO DAMN good.

I laid in bed, alone, but still feeling the aftershocks from the night prior.

Although Yusuf's revelation about his reason for being in Maui - to scatter his wife's ashes - brought me down every time I thought about it, thinking about the night before did the job of lifting me back up.

He left before sunrise, and right before I fell asleep. We went from the living room couch to my bedroom floor, sexing on repeat. Never tiring and only stopping to change positions. His stamina and agility were a complete match for mine. We were perfect like this... except for that *one* thing.

I sighed heavily, reaching for my phone on my night table.

I could put a lot out of my mind when we were in the act. Nothing else mattered when Yusuf and I were physical. It was nice. But as soon as I opened my eyes that morning, everything that happened at his condo before I left, and he followed me to mine, came rushing back to memory.

I wanted him again, though.

Phone in hand, I tapped into my social app.

I'd been lightly stalking his and his wife's social page.

See, that's the reason it's advised to stay clear of good dick. Because it will have you out here doing things like *lightly stalking*. Doing shit that makes you shake your head at your damn self.

But I was back on their social page, scrolling and scanning through square tiles in my attempt to find something, *anything*, to make me *not* want Yusuf inside me again later that day.

The urn and it being here should've done it. That should've been enough to back away and not even consider impeding.

Yusuf made me feel good, though. He made my time here better than I ever could have imagined. And the fact he considers me to be the same escape I consider him to be is more reason to link up with him later tonight.

Which, if I'm being honest, I was very excited to do.

I clicked on the first tile, a photo of the two of them. He wore a simple jeans and tee, and she did too, except she also wore a tiny white veil in her hair. She styled her hair into an easy top bun. Yusuf and Parris stood outside of a courthouse building, kissing. Her right foot lifted off the ground behind her. You know, like those animated drawings of women so in love and happy, it shows in their body language.

I pressed my hand to my chest, reading the caption, which was really an announcement about her sudden passing and Yusuf's love letter to her.

They were only words, but I could hear them in his voice. The pain, the shock, the disbelief in every sentence. Each word seemed carefully selected, properly organized, and so sincere it made my eyes well with tears.

"My goodness," I said low. "He really loved this woman."

Curiosity sent me to the comments. This whole time, I'd been returning to their social posts, only analyzing the photos, but I'd never peeked at the comments.

Because if I had, I would've remembered the feeling that came over me reading them.

Thinking I'd find only condolences and sincere remarks, there were comments from women offering to help Yusuf grieve. Commenting on how handsome he looked on their wedding day. Stating how they could understand why Parris looked so thrilled on those courthouse stairs.

They just seemed *so* inappropriate, tactless.

Where was the decorum?

This was a post announcing his wife's death, for goodness' sake.

The condolences and heartfelt remarks were more, but the few blaring but subtle sexual advances stood out to me.

And you know how negativity can sometimes be louder than positivity when you allow yourself to only see the negative.

Unfortunately, that's *all* I could see.

I couldn't unsee them.

They bothered me.

Annoyed me.

How dare these women think it's proper to lust after a man who is grieving his wife...

Like I was doing?

I laid my phone face down beside me on the bed and ran my hand over my face in reaction to that thought.

Was I doing that?

I knew he was grieving; he was hurting. He's told me his reason for being here, and I still wanted him. Every time Yusuf spoke of his wife and insisted on his feelings for her, it was clear his undying love would never change. And I still wanted him.

Even more.

Was that normal?

Where was *my* decorum?

I tossed the sheets off of me, grabbed my phone, and stepped off the bed, heading for my bathroom. I could still smell Yusuf's expensive cologne on my skin. So, I needed to get cleaned up… or wash myself of my sins?

"God," I sighed, getting beneath the shower head, allowing the beads of warm water to cascade down my limbs.

Leave it to me to find myself in a complicated situation while on vacation. I needed to talk to someone who I knew would be objective. And the only person I knew would know all about complicated situations was my childhood best friend Danyelle.

"Oh, *now* she calls me," she sassed when she answered on the second ring.

I giggled.

"Had my husband drop her ass to the airport—"

"Aht!" I scoffed. "You mean *my* brother?"

"I meant *my* husband."

I hollered a laugh.

Danyelle and my brother had been married for nine years. Before then, they carried on a secret relationship dating back to when Danyelle and I were thirteen. Danyelle would later reveal my brother was her first in everything. Things really got serious between them when I moved on campus at Brookville University. I was furious with them when the truth finally surfaced, but after a while; I realized I wouldn't have wanted it any other way. Danyelle was my sister, period. Not in law, just period. And I loved that for all of us.

"So, how is it?" She asked. "I'll take the CliffsNotes version. I'm about to load the kids into the car in a few minutes."

"It's beautiful," I started. "The weather is always perfect; the ocean view is everything."

"Then *why* do you sound like *that*?"

See why I called her?

Danyelle and I have known each other since we were in kindergarten. While others wouldn't have noticed anything, she always will.

"I done got myself into some shit out here, D." I confessed.

"Go on."

"I met a guy."

"Great!"

"He's a widower who traveled to the island *only* to scatter his wife's ashes."

"Gahdammit!"

"*Mm-hmm,*" I hummed. "Danyelle, I don't know what to do. He's great. We've been *hanging out*, and that's been great, too. But... he's got her ashes here and when we were in the middle of..."

"Hanging out," she finished.

"*Uh-huh.*" I snickered. "I noticed he had the urn here with him and that threw everything off, but it hasn't made me want him less. I want him *more*, but there's no way this thing between us can be anything other than what it is here on this island."

"But you want it to be more."

"Yeah, I think so."

She giggled. "Well, you know I know *all* about dealing with complicated shit with conflicting feelings of the heart."

"That's why I called you."

"*Oh,*" she stated dryly. "You called me for *that*? With your problems? Great. How lucky am I to have *that* privilege?"

I kissed my teeth. "Danyelle, quit, and tell me what you think I should do."

"I *think* you should just have fun like you have been doing," she offered. "That island is too damn beautiful for you to be over there, stressing over catching feelings for a man you met while on vacation. Live in the moment. And wherever that moment takes you, ride the wave. That's what I did... even though that wave is really calm right now."

"Really calm?" I arched a brow. "What do you mean by that? Did Clyde do something? You need me to speak to him?"

"No, do not speak to *my* husband." She laughed. "Clyde is great and always will be. He's just working a lot lately, which I can't complain about. Not having to stress over finances is the change I've prayed for. He's taking care of me and the kids. Grinding even with a new baby at home and with little sleep. I just... miss our little him and me time outside of our bedroom, is all." She sighed. "Forget I even said anything. I'm *just*... talking out loud."

I blinked a few times.

"Hey," she added, "Bring me back some of those Hawaiian cookies. I don't want a souvenir. Only the cookies. One girl in my mommy-and-me gymnastics class is always reminiscing about them when bragging about her little trip to Hawaii two summers ago, and I wanna know what all the fuss is about."

I smiled. "Done. I got you."

"Love you, Clarke," she told me. "And just have fun for the both of us over there, please."

"I love you too," I returned. "And I definitely will."

sixteen

CLARKE

JUST HAVE FUN.

That's what I kept reminding myself to do.

Laid out on the beach, Yusuf only an arm's reach away. Feeling the sun drench me in rays, and his eyes on me making me blush.

He called me about an hour after my shower earlier and my call with Danyelle. Invited me out to the resort's private beach.

We had activities planned with our Island Hop group. They were at the Nakalele Blowhole today and were visiting the Venus Pond, a natural pool with several waterfalls. The natural pool is connected to the ocean, so tiny waves made it into the pools, and it was a sight you just had to see - according to Patrice. Yusuf and I skipped all that to be alone.

Alone wasn't only us on the beach. People crowded the beach

that afternoon. Bikini and swim trunk clad beach goers toted surfboards tucked beneath their sunblock arms or headed toward the boat ride.

I laid face up on my beach towel, sunglasses shielding my eyes. I closed my lids and reveled in the moment. My pulse raced the second Yusuf brushed his thick lips against mine.

My lids lifted to find him comfortably in my space, firm hands grazing my abdomen as he attempted to get my attention...

... and my permission.

He scooted closer, burying his lips against my neck next.

I moaned, immediately turning to face him and cupping the back of his shaved head. And when he lifted his head enough for our lips to be aligned, I moved in for a kiss. He obliged. Parting my lips with his to take our kiss deep.

Real deep.

His arm stretched over my waist, hand clasping to the fullest part of my ass cheek, and he used his grip to draw me closer to him.

And I let him.

Because this felt good.

It felt right.

Our tongues swirled and twirled around one another as his brawny hands caressed my sun-warmed skin.

The seagulls's cries.

The undulating waves adding to the soundtrack of the moment.

Beachgoers surrounded Yusuf and me and there we were, on these people's beach, one kiss away from giving them a show.

Yusuf broke our kiss long enough to whisper, "Let's go," against my lips. "We need to take this indoors."

And you already know I didn't need to think twice about obeying that command.

My body tingled; nipples hardened. I moaned like I could already feel him inside me because I swore I could.

We quickly gathered our things and walked off the private beach hand in hand, kicking up sand as we exited as fast as we could.

My body was humming. Or maybe I was moaning with anticipation as we rode in the golf cart as he drove it to the cart rental stand close to our condominium village.

Inside the building that housed our condos and behind the chrome doors of the elevator alone, Yusuf and I kissed. My back up against the cool elevator wall, his warm body pressed to mine.

We moaned, growing more and more excited as the elevator climbed floors. He slid his hand into my swim skirt where it naturally divided to caress my pussy through my bathing suit's crotch.

"Yusuf, wait," I whispered, not wanting to do such a crazy thing like have sex on an elevator.

The elevator chimed with each floor as it ascended.

I looked up and into his eyes and he met my lusty gaze with one of his own, holding his bottom lip in the bite of his teeth as he ran his fingers up and down my heat that was getting so wet.

I gave in and rested the back of my head against the elevator's wall. Instead of resisting, I rolled my hips in time to his caresses until the elevator doors opened.

We were off the elevator by the time I realized we were heading to his condo.

I could think of nothing but getting behind his condo door.

And the moment we got inside, he took me in his arms, slamming his mouth into mine.

It was wild after that.

He untied the top of my bikini top, allowing my breasts to spill out.

"Damn Yusuf," I cried when he caught one of my nipples in his mouth. "Yes."

He carried me into his bedroom and balanced me in a seat on the console table beneath the mounted flatscreen.

Yusuf pulled his swim trunks off, stepping out of them, then quickly returned to flicking my nipple with his tongue. I tried to wiggle out of my bikini's bottom, but had little room to work with.

And I didn't want to interrupt how good he was making me feel doing what he was doing.

I grabbed at the side seam of my bikini's bottom and attempted to rock back and forth to get it off me, and when I did that, I heard something rocking on the table a few inches away from me.

Yusuf and I both heard it.

And when we glanced toward the noise, we gasped in absolute horror.

Because we saw when the purple and gold urn rocked back and forth on the table's surface, wobbling a little too hard to the right.

My eyes ballooned at the sight of it being so close to me and *so* close to tipping off the edge of that table.

I reached for it and so did he.

Thankfully, he had longer arms and moved faster because he caught it as it was about to fall off the table and land on his bedroom's floor.

I slapped my hands to my mouth, watching as his chest heaved up and down uncontrollably.

"I'm sorry, Parris," he whispered to the urn. "I'm sorry baby."

He kept repeating that.

Kept chanting it to the urn as if it were a person. As if it had feelings.

Like I wasn't sitting there, with my titties out, feeling out of place and confused.

"You should go," he suggested, eyes still fixed on the urn as he positioned it farther up on the console table.

"Are... are you talking to *me* now?"

After I said that, I realized it sounded *very* insensitive.

But... I was *so* confused and a little... jealous, if I'm being honest.

Clarke, are you really jealous of an urn?

No, I'm *jealous* of his undying loyalty to a woman who's no longer here.

I'm *here* though. With my titties out and his dick in clear view... and he's asking *me* to leave.

I draped an arm over my breasts and hopped off the console table.

"Clarke, I'm sorry," he apologized. "This just... we almost knocked over—"

"I get it." I turned to face him when I arrived at the bedroom's doorway. I shrugged next. "You love your wife."

He swallowed hard in response.

I glanced out of the room to see my bikini top on the floor and puffed my cheeks with air before blowing it out slow.

So much for just having fun.

I left, not saying another word. Because there was nothing to say.

He loved his wife.

And that would not change. Nor should it.

We'd only known each other for all of a week.

His reaction shouldn't have bothered me.

But it did, and I couldn't help but to feel really hurt by that fact.

And I couldn't understand how I accidentally was playing the role of the other woman yet again.

seventeen

YUSUF

DAMN... *I can't believe I almost let that happen yesterday.*

Can't believe I haven't left my condo since yesterday, either.

I lounged out on the patio, reclined all the way back as my eyes danced along the clear blue skies overhead.

Yesterday's events played on in my mind on repeat, making me cringe each time my recollection brought me back to the very moment my wife's ashes almost fell to my bedroom floor.

How horrified I would've been to have to sweep her ashes up to pour back into her urn. Parts of her, at least. Because there is no way I'd get all of her ashes off that floor.

I kissed my teeth and squeezed my eyelids shut.

I was so fucking disappointed in myself.

Disappointed I almost had sex with another woman inches away from my wife's urn. Disappointed I allowed myself to get to that level of comfort to do it to begin with.

Disappointed in how I made Clarke feel because of it all.

She didn't deserve any of what she felt, but... I didn't know any other way to deal.

I hadn't called her room, hadn't left my condo to engage with anyone except for room service to accept my food and drink orders.

I was still processing.

My cellphone rang with a call. When I lifted the device's screen within view, my heart sank at the name that appeared on it.

"Fuck," I whispered, sitting up from my recline, clearing my throat to get it together before answering.

"Mama T." I smiled easily.

"Yusuf."

Her voice was so sing-songy and warm, like always.

"Only three more days," she announced. "Are you ready? How are you?"

I shut my lids and held them tightly together.

Three more days until Parris's birthday.

Three more days until I had to do what I came here to do.

Scatter her ashes.

Leave without the urn.

"Yusuf, honey? Are you there?"

I cleared my throat again. "Yeah, yeah, Mama T." I nodded like she could see me. "I'm right here."

Parris's mother, Mrs. Tawanna Cole, insisted I call her Mama T when I greeted her by Mrs. Tawanna when we first met. She hated it. Laughed for a good minute. I'd only met *her*. Parris's father died six years before Parris and I met.

Mama T welcomed me with open arms when Parris brought me home to meet her. She had Parris ask me from ahead of time what my favorite meal was so she could cook it.

Although my mother was just as loving, it was great having two women in my life who loved me as their son.

The embarrassment and disappointment that has been weighing me down grew a few pounds heavier hearing her voice on my line.

"I know it's hard," she started. "When Parris's father died, there wasn't anything anyone could say to me to make me think things would get better or that I would ever feel better. You already had to say goodbye to her once and now you have to do it again when you scatter her ashes, I get it."

"Nothing could ever compare to losing a child," I remarked low. "It's you I should say this to. It's *you* I should be comforting."

"Oh, Yusuf, give yourself some grace, my love."

I shook my head.

Because it was so much more than that. I didn't deserve to have her speak so understandingly to me. Not after the shit I've been doing out here. Not staying focused. Losing all sense of control. I almost knocked Parris's ashes to the fucking floor while I was about to fuck another woman right beside her.

I wasn't thinking.

"I wish I had someone who understood and could tell me everything would be okay all those years back when Parris's father passed." She chuckled lowly. "So, I wouldn't have felt like I was the only person on the planet who lost someone they thought they'd live forever with."

"Hmph."

"Because life goes on," she continued. "It has to."

But I don't want it to.

I didn't say that out loud, though. But it was true.

"Now I hope you've been at least enjoying yourself over there."

I reclined in the patio lounge chair.

"I know you said you were going out there with a group."

"*Mm-hmm.*"

"Hope you've been *actually* going out with them."

I sighed.

"Be around people, Yusuf," she advised. "I know it's hard to see that as necessary, but please get out a little in the next few days. Definitely before you have to scatter her ashes."

"I've gotten *out* enough," I rasped, trying to hold back my tears, but failing miserably. "I just... I want to do what I came here to do and come back home."

"Oh, Yusuf." She sniffled. "I wish I could hug you, let you know everything will be just fine."

I ran my hand down my face to catch the tears before they could fall. "I could use one of your hugs right now."

We were quiet for a few minutes. Mama T broke the silence by saying, "Thank you for flying all that way to give my baby her last wish. You're such a good man. You're a great husband."

I snatched the phone from my ear and dropped my head back against the lounge chair, banging the back of my head against it twice.

The phone was back to my ear when I told her, "Don't mention it."

And I meant that. I didn't want her to mention it because I *wasn't* a good man.

Definitely not a good husband.

Not in my eyes.

Because there wasn't anything good about me and what I've done these past few days.

But I would fix it, by staying focused and on task... and avoiding Clarke.

Even though she helped take my mind off something that had been bringing me down for a while now, nothing good could come from something so temporary and so unplanned.

CLARKE

I LISTENED to the phone trill out for the third time.

When it was clear Yusuf would not answer, I scoffed and slammed the cordless phone against its base, then stood up out of my seat at the work desk to step out onto the patio.

Him not answering would've made me concerned. The last time I spoke with Yusuf was the day we almost knocked his wife's ashes over in the middle of us initiating sex. Since then, I'd been calling and getting no response. Probably would've thought to get someone at the resort to pay his condo a wellness visit, except the concierge confirmed she'd seen him earlier that morning... and the day before that.

"He's ghosting me," I surmised, dropping myself onto the lounge chair and dropping my head back against the low back. *"He's ghosting me?"*

He'd have to be.

I hadn't spoken to Yusuf and Yusuf hadn't bothered reaching out to me. And although I understood I should've viewed his decision to create distance between us as a wise one, given the complexity of the situation, I didn't feel too great about him ignoring my calls to his condo's phone or his failure to reach out to me after everything.

There were only a few days left of my trip.

I thought about linking up with my Island Hop group to take part in the final few group activities, but I was over it.

Not over Hawaii. This place, despite my current focuses, was a magical oasis. I was over this solo thing. And I didn't feel like interacting with my boring ass group. Touring the island with a group just wasn't as fun or sexy as it was experiencing the island with only Yusuf.

I shook my head at myself.

Here I was, again.

My cellphone rang, and I quickly snatched it up off the chair's cushion. Yusuf didn't have my cellphone number but my mind was still on him, and for a moment, I hoped he'd somehow gotten my device's number and had called me here.

But it was my grandmother.

"Hey, Nana," I greeted when I answered.

"Hey baby," she replied with enthusiasm. Enthusiasm I couldn't muster up. "How are you? How's the island?"

I shifted my focus to out in front of me at the view. "Hawaii is as beautiful as the day I landed."

"Then why do you sound like it somehow took off its mask and it ain't as cute as it was when you arrived?"

I sighed. "Because I'm letting a man ruin my time, yet again."

"What's going on?"

"I met someone, Nana," I revealed. "An incredible man, with an even more incredible heart, and I like him. I like him a lot. And I wasn't sure before, but now I know for a fact this is feeling like more than just a vacation fling."

"Oh, my goodness," she exclaimed slowly. "God actually listens to me when I ask for things."

I laughed. "Oh, so I have you to blame for this?"

"Blame?" She giggled. "Based on what you've told me, I don't see a problem."

"It's the guy from the plane. He isn't married, nor is he here on vacation," I told her. "He's a widower, and he flew to Maui specifically to scatter his wife's ashes. The man is here with his wife's ashes, Nana."

"Oh, shoot," she whispered. "My prayer wasn't specific enough."

I hollered a laugh, a laugh I really needed.

"Him being here with her ashes and that being the only reason he's here is something I was coping with, you know?" I spoke. "But now he's not answering any of my phone calls, and my pride is too big for me to go to his doorstep."

"The grieving process when you lose a spouse is very difficult, Clarke," she explained. "We all think about happily ever after and don't consider what happens when the other half of the happily ever after departs."

I inhaled a deep breath, then let it go slowly.

"When your grandfather died, I felt like I'd lost the feeling in a limb," she revealed. "He was the love of my life. *My* person. We had the life insurance. We had things set in place for his death. But even when you're prepared, you can never really prepare for the people you love to die."

"Yeah. I can empathize with that part." I nodded. "I'm just... I'm *so* tired. I'm tired of falling for men who are emotionally unavailable. And at one point, I thought it was just men who couldn't commit. Who didn't know how to be loyal and to keep the promises they made. But here is a man, who was married, loved his wife until the day she died, but he can't let her go and it shows, but I still want him."

"*Mm-hmm,*" Nana agreed.

"I should've stuck to my original plan when I came here." I moved my eyes along the grounds of the resort, taking in all that was around me. "I should've come here, only focused on doing the group activities and made this trip about *me*. But *nooo,*" I dragged out. "Clarke just had to fly her ass over 4,000 miles to another part of the country, only to do the same shit she always does. Fall for men who aren't emotionally available, but this time with an island twist. A man who's as in love with his dead wife as he was when she was alive, God." I grunted. "I'm really here on the last few days of my vacation, obsessing over a man—"

"Has it ever occurred to you, beautiful granddaughter of mine," Nana cut in, "that the two of you meeting on that there island is divine purpose and you may be there for *him*? Because maybe he needs you more than you may think?"

That shut me right up.

"I love you, baby, but sometimes you can be quite frustrating."

I sputtered a laugh. "Damn, Nana. Tell me how you really feel. Don't hold back."

"I never do."

I laughed out loud this time.

"You're always trying to control how life gives you a gift," she continued. "You can't control that. You do it with everything. You wanna tell me every time you leave my home for me not to die while you're away. I get that it's tied to you being away on a trip when your granddaddy died. I get it."

I inhaled deeply, remembering that time.

"But me transitioning is going to benefit you. And you're going to love it."

"Nana, what the hell you talkin' over there?"

"I'm leaving the vineyard to you in my Will."

I sat up immediately. "Excuse me?"

"The vineyard in Napa will be yours when I pass. I had transfer of ownership and control paperwork finalized soon after I realized your father would not take over the business and when I realized how much you loved that vineyard."

"But Nana." I shook my head. I couldn't believe what I was hearing. "I thought you sold it. Dad said you did five years ago, after your stroke."

"I told *him* I sold it because I didn't want *him* selling it," she admitted. "I hired people to handle all the operations, from harvesting to management. That's it. It's still mine. I still own it and it will all be yours when I'm gone. That way, when your father finds out at the Will reading, I'll be long gone and won't have to hear him fuss about it. Thank God."

I laughed, then held the smile on my lips.

"Still don't want me to die, Clarke?"

"Nana." I giggled. "Of course, I still don't. But... at least it won't be *so* bad when you do, I guess."

She cackled, which made me laugh some more.

"I know how much you hate that office you work in. I've noticed how out of love you've fallen with the idea of practicing law. Baby, follow your dreams. Live the life you want to love."

I nodded slowly.

"Regarding this man you've met, you may not have met him when your situations were picture perfect, but you have to see beyond the attachment you have to your ideals. Sometimes they aren't realistic. Sometimes they don't serve you well in every situation. You must learn to adjust and shift the way you perceive how life wraps your gifts. Sometimes they don't have pretty little bows around them. A lot of times they don't even look like gifts, and you know what? That's okay."

I nodded.

"Because let me tell you something. Life is more about how you respond to it and less about what happens *in* it. Quit thinking only about yourself here and what's happening to you, Clarke, please," she encouraged. "You wanted a great man who you wanted to believe could be faithful. And voila! You attracted his energy. You attracted a man who is exactly what you said you wanted, just packaged differently but still positioned in your path. What are you going to do now that you've finally found him?"

* * *

I had a lot to think about. A lot to process after my phone call with Nana.

I didn't want to spend the rest of my time in my condo, so I grabbed the blanket at my condo, took a walk to the resort's private beach, and grabbed a seat on the sand to watch the sunset by the ocean.

It wasn't as beautiful as viewing the sunset from the top of the volcano at Haleakala National Park, but it was still a gorgeous sight to behold.

My thoughts kept wandering to Yusuf, though. As hard as I tried not to think of him, I couldn't help it.

I missed him.

A lot.

His company was something I'd gotten used to in Maui.

Gotten used to it, period, if I'm being honest.

And after the conversation I had with Nana, I was now positive this thing between us was feeling like something more than just a vacation thing.

My phone chimed with a call. It was my brother.

"Hey Clyde."

"What's going on?" He asked. The gentle cooing of my baby nephew in the call's background immediately melted my heart.

"Watching the sunset on the most beautiful island in the world," I answered. "You know, the usual."

He chuckled lowly. "Could use that kind of usual right about now."

"I bet." I smiled. "It's after midnight in New York and Baby Clyde doesn't sound like he's ready for bed."

"Not at all. This guy is wide awake. So, it's gonna be me, him, and Netflix for the next hour or two. Ain't that right?"

The sound of my brother kissing my nephew brought another smile to my face.

"I'm calling to find out if you'll need to be picked up from the airport," he informed. "You know how I *hate* last-minute favors so I'm trying to get ahead of things 'cause I know how you do."

"You know me well." I giggled. "I might. I'll let you know."

"Cool."

"Hey Clyde?"

"Yeah?"

"Buy Danyelle some flowers and take her out some place nice."

There was silence on the line for a beat before he told me, "That's very random."

"I spoke with her a few days ago and she may have suggested she misses you two's alone time."

He sighed. "Things have been a little busy around here with Baby Clyde here now and me needing to work more. But... we still have our time. I still make time for us."

"Dude, sex is not enough, okay?"

"Wow," he exclaimed.

"It's true though," I doubled down. "I know you two are never not having sex. You have three kids and she already told me she looks forward to the nighttime because that's when she gets to *play* with her husband. I wish she didn't tell me that, but here I am with information I don't want."

"Danyelle tells you too damn much."

"You two have to spend time together independent of the kids and of a bed," I told him. "You know I'm here and would be happy to spend time with my nieces and nephew. You can find time between work and other things to hang out with your wife. Take her out on a date. Show her a good time. She misses it. She misses you."

"How are *you* telling me things about *my* wife?"

"She's *my* sister and *my* best friend, and when you two started getting it on behind my back..."

"Here you go."

"... I told you that you better treat her right and not mess things up," I added, "because she means the world to me and so do you. And I've realized in conversation with Nana and some things I learned here in Maui that memories built with a spouse is the only thing of real value you get to keep and that no one can *ever* take from you when they're dead and gone."

"Whoa! *Dead and gone*?" He said loud. "The fuck you on right now, Clarke?!"

"Exactly," I voiced. "Didn't consider death now, did you?"

He was quiet for a moment.

"Work will be work. The kids will grow up and leave the house wanting to have their own lives. Make time to nurture what you have with Danyelle."

"That's real," he agreed.

"Because I know you didn't betray me, getting with my best friend behind my back, only to drop the ball, right?"

He laughed. "I'm gonna hear about this damn dramatic ass betrayal story for the rest of my life."

"Oh, of course." I smiled. "Y'all gave me beautiful nieces and a handsome nephew, but I'll forever have a gripe with you two for keeping your love a secret from me and for so long."

"*Mm-hmm*." He snickered. "You're right though. About nurturing what Danyelle and I have. Not the whole secret thing. You need to get over that, for real."

I rolled my eyes playfully.

"I'll take care of her. That woman is my everything," he confirmed. "I'll do a better job of showing that more than saying it."

"Thank you."

"Nah, Clarke, *thank you*."

I smiled big. "Always."

nineteen

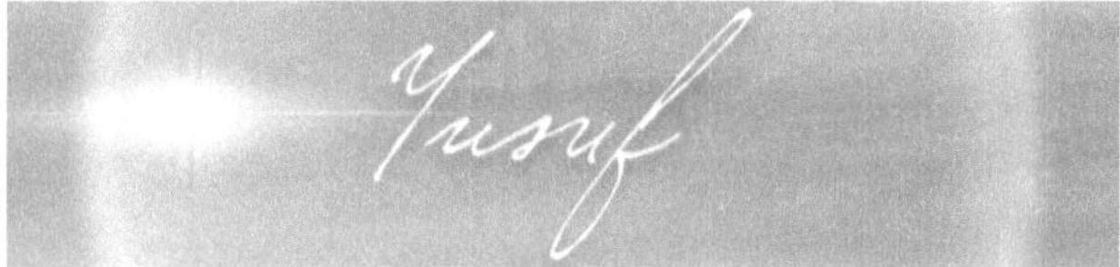

YUSUF

I DIDN'T GET any sleep the night before.

I hadn't been getting much sleep since the whole knocking the urn situation but, the closer the days got to Parris's heavenly birthday, the less rest I got.

The condo was where I planned to spend the day, again.

I'd only left my condo to get food the day before and the day before that.

With plans to do the same thing, I was sliding my feet into a pair of flip-flops when my cellphone vibrated in my pocket.

It was Mama T.

Our conversation two days ago was a quick one. She promised she'd call me again to check in on me.

"I was hoping you'd sound different today," she said when she answered.

This call was a video call, so I got to see her youthful grin and hear her voice.

"And you don't look too good," she added. "You've been sleeping?"

"Barely," I answered, taking a seat on the couch.

"My goodness." She frowned. "Yusuf, is this how it's been since you've been there?"

I closed my eyes, then ran my hand down my mouth.

"What?" she questioned. "What's that look about?"

"I haven't been completely honest."

She tilted her head to one side.

"And... it doesn't feel too good keeping things from you."

"Keeping what from me?" She asked.

The last thing I wanted to do was tell her. But I also could not lie either.

"When I... *ummm*... flew out here, I met a woman on the flight." I looked away from the phone, so I didn't have to see her face. "It wasn't intentional, at first. She just kept popping up wherever I was and ended up being in the same travelers group as me. We got to know each other and realized we had a lot in common." I bit inside my cheek. "The getting to know one another eventually got physical."

"Oh," she chimed in. "Okay."

"I've stopped seeing her though," I insisted, refocusing on the screen. "I haven't called her, haven't been out of my rental condo, so I haven't run into her—"

"Well..." She smiled. "Why would you do something terrible like that?"

"I know, I'm sorry." I released a stuttering exhale. "I got caught up in the environment. Got caught up in her carefreeness and lost sight of why I'm here—"

"No, Yusuf, not *why* would you spend time with another

woman," she clarified. "I meant, *why* would you stop speaking to her?"

I stared at her smiling face on the screen.

"You meeting someone else is a good thing, Yusuf," she told me. "It's a great thing, son."

My brows knitted over my eyes.

"And the fact it's happened during one of the most difficult times for you... it's God." She giggled a little. "Probably even Parris."

That took me aback.

"You know, the girl used to love to be in control of everything." Mama T tucked her lips into her mouth to keep from laughing. "It wouldn't shock me one bit that she worked her Parris magic and sent this woman to you somehow. What are the chances? You delay going over there last year only to go now and meet someone on the flight over? Someone who you really like?"

I shook my head. "I don't know about that.

"Yusuf—"

"I feel awful," I exhaled. "I've been feeling awful for days."

"And Parris would not have wanted that."

Tears began welling in my eyes and I shut my lids tight to keep them in.

"She would not have wanted you to feel miserable through all of this. She loved you just like you loved her."

"I wouldn't have wanted her to do this," I confessed. "Come to an island to do something for me, but then fall for another guy? No way."

"I don't believe that," she said back. "I think you would've wanted her to be happy too, if you had the choice. Yusuf, you have nothing to feel bad about, hear me?"

I rested the back of my head against the couch's pillows.

"You have done *nothing* wrong. Parris is gone, and it breaks my heart like it breaks your heart to accept this. But it is true."

I sighed.

"And you're young. *Very* young. You still have a lot of life in you,

God willing. Do not spend another minute feeling like you're wrong for moving on. That's what you're supposed to do. I sure wish I did."

I lifted my head to meet her eyes on the screen.

"If I could go back, I would've probably put myself out there." She nodded. "I would've grieved for however long I needed to, and I would've started dating again. Absolutely. I'm doing it now. It took Parris passing away for me to see and know for certain I want more connections in my life. I want to meet as many people as possible and learn their stories because we all have one. And I'm fascinated by that."

"That's great, Mama T," I said low. "You deserve to get out and do what will make you happy."

"And you, too." She winked. "Yusuf, you will always be my son. Nothing is going to change that. Parris brought you into my life and here you will stay, unconditionally."

My bottom lip trembled as I tried to keep my emotions from welling even more in my eyes.

"Everyone deserves romantic love after loss. Do not deprive yourself of it because you think that's what you're supposed to do. No," she remarked. "You are still here. Stop punishing yourself for that. And with each day you have breath in your body, you owe it to yourself, you owe it to Parris, and you owe it to God to live the life you still have."

Each word hit me hard in the chest. It was the talk I needed. The talk my therapist has been sweetly having with me, but Mama T, as always, gave it to me with a heavy dose of honesty.

"Tomorrow is going to be hard for you," she forecasted. "Your heart is going to break all over again. You shouldn't feel any of that alone, Yusuf. Please."

"I hear you Mama T," I acknowledged. "But I don't have a choice on that. Alone is the only way I want to do this."

twenty

CLARKE

THE MOMENT I got to Makena State Park Little Beach, the beach Yusuf mentioned when telling me about his plans to scatter his wife's ashes, I stopped to scan the surrounding area. I hoped I got there in time and didn't miss him. I'd missed sunrise by a few minutes, having caught the shuttle late due to my indecisiveness regarding going, but I figured I'd take a chance, anyway.

I moved my eyes around the landscape closest to me.

Few people were on the beach at that hour.

The area was fairly empty, with a handful of people spread out here and there.

I spotted him almost immediately, standing not too far from where I entered, and away from everyone else.

I noticed his shoulders. I could pick them out in a lineup.

He wore a cotton tee, basketball shorts, and sneakers. I did the same, except my shorts were denim.

I took a chance coming out. I wasn't sure if it was appropriate to be here or if he would want to see me when he was doing something so intimate. Fulfilling a promise to his wife. But last night I told myself I would get on the resort's shuttle and take it out here so he wouldn't have to be alone.

He may not have asked for my support, but I wanted to offer it to him, anyway.

Even if it was way out of my comfort zone.

Because my grandmother was right. I asked for a man like Yusuf. I wanted a man like him minus the deceased wife thing, but he was here. And though I didn't plan to meet a man like him here while on vacation, I would not pass him up just because he wasn't the plan.

The closer to him I got, the more movement I saw on those shoulders. And the more space I closed between us, I realized they were shaking from him crying.

"Oh my God," I said to myself, pressing my hand to my heart.

The sky was a beautiful orange, yellow, red. The rays that dispersed from the sun and colored the clouds in a hue I've never seen, looked as if the sunrise were serving as a portal that led to a place beyond the clouds.

I was within feet of him when I noticed the purple and gold urn without its lid. A closer look showed it was empty inside.

"Yusuf," I called when I was within feet of him.

He turned his head toward my voice. His face was wet with tears. He dropped his head for a moment, swiped a hand down his face, then looked to me again.

"Hey," he rasped.

My heart broke at the defeated look in his eyes, the sag in his posture and the grief in his tone.

I approached him and pulled him into a hug. I felt when he let his weight go on me, just a little. Yusuf held me tight against him, sniffled twice when I ran my hand up and down his back as he buried his face into my locs.

"Thank you," he whispered to me before kissing me on the cheek and gently pulling away.

We stood there for a minute or two, saying nothing after.

"It wasn't as hard as I thought it would be," he told me, eyes fixed on the ocean water. "I was fine until I looked inside the urn and realized it was now empty." He shook his head. "Lost it after that."

I rubbed his back because it was the only thing I knew to do.

"She's really gone now, one with the ocean and the sunrise, like she's always wanted."

"My grandmother said something profound when I told her about you and your loss."

A small smile pulled at his lips. "Telling your family about me now?"

"Oh, of course." I smiled back. "When you meet an amazing man while on vacation, you gotta tell everyone who will listen about him. Those are the rules."

Yusuf half smiled. "Of course."

"Nana, my grandmother, follows the thinking that we are not our bodies. We're in them for a limited time. Well, she started thinking *that way* after she lost my grandfather five years ago."

Yusuf turned to face me.

"She said when you shift your perception to the understanding you are life without boundaries, you'll realize you are energy. Energy that can exist for however long people have memories of you. And I agree."

"Hmph." He nodded, looking out into the ocean.

"Parris isn't gone," I volunteered, laying my hand against his heart. "She'll always be *right here*, and in everything and everywhere you remember her being. Her energy is here in Maui, in the song you two loved, in the food that was your favorites. She's in *everything*. And even though she may not be here in the physical, she will always be in whatever way you choose to remember her. Because you'll remember her more *as* she was than *what* she was in the physical. You'll remember her energy most of all. And energy never dies."

He stared at me for a long while, before wrapping an arm around my shoulders and bringing me closer to him and into his space.

Yusuf tilted my head back by my chin and told me, "You're really a blessing, Clarke. Not just to me. You're a blessing, *period*."

And I swore I could've melted into the sand because of the way he looked at me when he spoke those words.

Yusuf stared into my eyes, his gaze soft before he sighed in defeat and closed his eyes for only a moment.

"I know," I said to him. "Trust me, *I* know what you're feeling." I smiled up at him. "You didn't come here for this."

"I didn't come here for this," he parroted.

"For whatever this is between us."

"At all," he concurred.

"Tell me about it." I shrugged. "Neither did I."

"I came to scatter my wife's ashes."

"I came to escape and to get away from married men." I pursed my lips together. "Couldn't even do that right. Clearly."

He snorted then gave into a deep hearty laugh that made me giggle in response.

"You make me feel good, though." He brushed his thumb down my chin. "Really, *really* good. Something I haven't felt in a while."

"Same."

Yusuf brushed his thumb over my bottom lip, then leaned in and kissed me.

And I kissed him back.

Everything muting around us until all I could hear was our breathing as we allowed ourselves to get lost in the moment.

He broke our kiss long enough to tell me, "Come on."

Yusuf threaded his fingers with mine as we walked off the beach and toward the resort's shuttle, leaving the urn in the sand.

The ride back was more of a relief than the ride to the beach.

Returning to the resort and to his condo felt... different.

A good different.

There was no hesitation between us this time when Yusuf took me in his arms and kissed me with the type of affection that made it seem air wasn't that important to him.

Because like me he wanted to be in the now, and nothing else mattered but what we were doing.

Our clothes came off with ease, no rush.

In fact, the entire act, once we got into our rhythm, was slow.

So sensual.

A lot of kissing, more touching. We actually took our clothes off this time. And I know that wasn't a big deal, but it was different. A different I could truly feel.

Yusuf's lips never left my skin as we sexed. Kissing me from my lips to my neck, and my neck to my shoulders before trailing his lips up to mine again. We rarely changed positions because we didn't want to interrupt the sweet connection we'd created with our lazy movements.

When we came, we came together. The pulsing rush building gradually to the point I didn't expect it to peak. But when it did, he moaned deeply with me as if he were feeling what I was experiencing. Eyes opened, hands caressing and gripping for leverage, breaths in sync and echoing our duet of moans.

"Oh my God, Yusuf," I exhaled in a long stream of air and closed my eyes when I collided with my climax.

Yusuf threaded his fingers with mine to keep me still as he stroked me through my release.

This was heaven.

Whatever *this* was between us.

And while the old me would run from anything I couldn't label, anything that made little sense. There with Yusuf, on that bed with him between my thighs making me feel more than the whirlwind sensation of coming, I wanted to stay in whatever it was we'd found on the island of Maui forever... and a day.

* * *

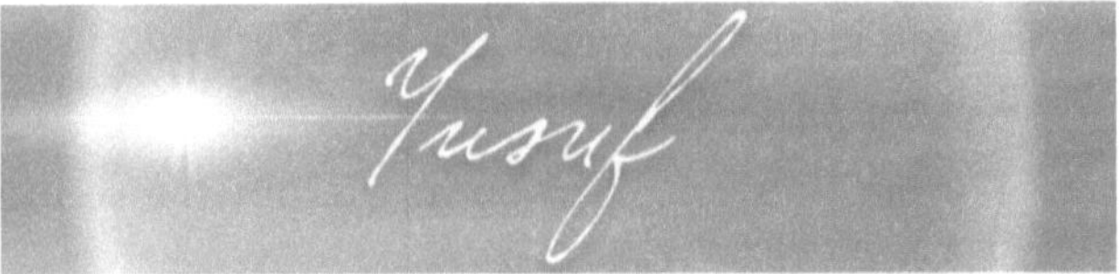

YUSUF

"I already know what seat you want," I teased, smiling as Clarke and I arrived at our aisle.

"As long as you know," she said behind me.

We were boarding our flight back to New York City.

The feeling I had leaving Maui was nothing like how I felt when I landed.

On arrival, I was so uncertain, anxious, and not looking forward to landing on the island of memories. On departure, I was flying back to New York City filled with immense hope and gratitude.

If someone would've told me the woman who gave me attitude on my flight to Maui would be a woman, I'd eventually change my flight to fly back with to New York, I wouldn't have believed them and I would've had a good laugh at that.

I'd planned to return to New York the same day I scattered Parris's ashes. When I initially booked my round-trip flight, I didn't know my trip would take the turn it did... for the better. Because I wanted to scatter her ashes and hightail off that island. Figured I wouldn't want to remain in Maui after emptying my wife's urn. So, I planned to return to New York hours later that day.

But then Clarke showed up.

And set fire to my plans.

I smiled to myself as I placed her bag in the overhead bin and then mine.

My carryon was lighter with the urn gone. Leaving it on the beach was something I planned to do, although parting ways with the vase I'd been talking to for a little over a year was easier to do with Clarke present. Having Clarke at the beach yesterday to help me process everything was a blessing I didn't even know I needed.

"Thank you." She sidestepped out of the aisle as she moved to claim the window seat.

I took her hand when I took my seat beside her, in the aisle seat, threading my fingers with hers, then lifting our interlocked hands to kiss the back of her palm.

Passengers continued to board the flight to New York City, some of them passing us on their way to their seats.

"I'm glad you stayed an extra day to fly out with me." She bit her lip and rested her chin on my shoulder. "Last night was..."

"Everything," I finished, flashing a smile.

"And more," she added, dropping her forehead to hide her shy smile.

I laughed in reaction.

Last night was nice. Genuinely good all around.

The sex, of course, was great. Sex was always an exciting experience with her. But it was the talking and building afterwards that brought me satisfaction sex couldn't provide.

"I want to see you after Maui, Clarke."

We laid in my bed covered only in white sheets. A soft afternoon breeze swept in through my opened patio door, filling the brief silence between us.

Clarke was resting in my arms when she looked up at me with curiosity in her eyes at what I'd said.

"Are you sure?"

I nodded. "Yes. Definitely."

She licked her lips and draped her arm over my abdomen. "Do you think you're ready for that? Seeing me after Maui?"

"I want you, Clarke."

"Oh, you want me?"

I tightened my grip around her waist. "Very much so."

"Well, I want you too." She smiled. "Very much so as well."

I leaned close to kiss her forehead, which made her moan.

"I want to ask you something." I slid my arm free from around her so I could turn to face her completely.

"Okay..." I noticed the moment her expression shifted from pleased to worry. *"What do you want to ask me?"*

"You've been fantastic to me, Clarke. There for me in ways I didn't know I needed, and that I never expected. But I don't want things to feel one-sided between us. I'm used to giving more than taking in my relationships, and it's been a while since I've been able to give. I want to give again."

Her brows wrinkled.

"I believe in filling the cup that pours into me." I ran my fingers through her locs and she closed her eyes to my touch. *"Balance is a priority to me. It was in my marriage. It is in my life."*

She nodded.

"I want to be there for you the same way you've been there for me... in whatever way that makes you feel you have the support you never thought you needed, too. I want to double your effort. Because you've made me feel really good again. And I want to make you feel great."

She released a long exhale and giggled nervously. "Okay, so this is a pleasant convo?"

I laughed. "Definitely."

"For a second there, I thought you were about to hit me with something unpleasant. And trust me, I've had enough unpleasant to last a lifetime."

I caressed the side of her cheek. "No, beautiful. I want our paradise to extend beyond Maui. That's all."

She smiled. "Communication, appreciation, and transparency are all very sexy to me," she revealed. "Any way you can express that you're thinking about me, even if it's just a text checking in, I'll appreciate it. Just don't shut down and ghost me again."

"I won't."

"I understand needing the space and time to process what you're dealing with, but tell me that. I'm not clingy or someone who doesn't understand needing space. I'll give you the time you need to yourself and

will be there when you're ready. Just... communicate that to me. I swear I'll listen."

"Communication, appreciation, and transparency, and always show you ways you're on my mind." I nodded slowly. "I can come through with all those things and more."

We stayed in bed and talked for hours after, getting to know each other even better, also sharing more about our lives in New York.

Of course, that won't be enough. I honestly don't know what lies ahead for Clarke and me, but I was ready to explore it.

"What are your plans after we land?" She asked.

"I'd love to take you to dinner," I replied without missing a beat. "Take you to my favorite Brazilian spot in Tribeca. Or order in. Something. Anything. Nothing too much since I'm sure we'll experience jet lag. I usually need a day to get my body back in sync with the eastern time zone."

She batted her pretty lashes.

"How does dinner sound... in whatever way we decide to have it?"

"Like you're trying to take up all my time." She scooted closer and pressed her lips against mine. "And I love that for me."

"I love that for *us*," I told her, gently parting her lips with mine in a kiss. Willfully retreating into a world I never thought I'd ever want to get lost in.

A world where love showed the potential of thriving after loss.

epilogue

CLARKE

I WAITED in line at a local cafe for the two cups of Americano coffee I ordered on arrival.

Snow flurries melted into my wool coat under the cafe's heat.

Seven days after the New Year, New York City was experiencing its third straight day of snow.

White blanketed the city's sidewalks. Wherever car wheels rolled laid various shades of slush brown dirt mixed into the snow.

The days were colder lately, but my bed was always warm, especially with Yusuf in it.

After returning from our trip to Maui, we didn't waste any time making things official. The plan was for us to take it easy. To let life unfold in the way it wanted to naturally.

But... the natural for us was stating what we desired, and that was each other.

So, we officially started our relationship in August, shortly after we returned from Maui, and it had been blissful living ever since.

"Small caramel latte," the barista shouted behind the counter.

Patrons crowded the cafe, but the cafe was large enough to accommodate us all. I didn't imagine I'd be here long, anyway.

Besides my love life, life did a complete 180 after I landed back in New York.

I still worked as a paralegal at the law firm I've been working at for years, but I've stopped studying for the bar.

A revelation that disappointed my parents. But Nana has calmed those waters, telling them affirmatively to, *"stay your esquired asses out of my baby's life. She can do what she wants, just like you two have. Live your life and let her live hers."*

I haven't heard a criticism since.

It was her telling me I was in line to inherit her vineyard that made me course correct. I couldn't keep the news to myself, telling my brother of course, and he has had dreams of a vineyard and farm-to-table restaurant plan that has given both of us an exciting vision of growing the family business together.

Instead of studying for the bar, I've been studying to become a sommelier. I'm about to be in the wine production business. It only seemed right I finally do what I've always dreamed of doing... traveling the world and drinking wine... even though a sommelier did far more than that.

Truthfully, juggling both working as a paralegal and researching all the right steps to doing what I've wanted to do since I was eighteen has been challenging, but I love it. Love it more than law. So, the joy from it has soothed the challenges of it all as I walked on this new journey of living the life I want to love.

"Large black coffee," the barista shouted next.

After the cafe, I planned to meet up with Yusuf. He told me to keep my Sunday free because he had something special planned and needed me to be there. He'd texted me an address of a hotel near Central Park and the knowledge we'd be meeting up at a hotel in a few has kept me feeling warm all over in this city chill.

We've been inseparable since we returned from Maui. Dinner that night became breakfast the next morning, then lunch on my lunch break, when I returned to work later that week.

We spoke on the phone for hours, sharing likes and dislikes, debating on what's better about everything from cereal to movies.

The challenges have been there. Like the disagreement we had over his insistence of me meeting Parris's mother when he brought me home to meet his family. I initially said no. I felt the whole thing would be so awkward, but he explained his reasoning behind it.

"She is a part of my family," he told me as we relaxed across from each other in his Brooklyn condo. "She loves me without conditions and is a part of a past I want you to know about. I want you to know every part of me." He took my hand and kissed the back of it. *"But if you don't want to, if the whole thing makes you uncomfortable. I won't push the issue. I just want you to know all of me and everyone I love, and Mama T is a part of my unique tribe I consider blessings."*

I couldn't say no after that. It's like I said, transparency just did something for me, and Yusuf let me into his heart with no limitations. He challenged me to be a little less selfish and to step out of my comfort zone with everything. And often when I did, I learned something valuable that changed me a little and always for the best.

Parris's mom, who insisted I *also* call her Mama T, when we met, reminded me of Nana, only younger.

When we first met, her first words to me warmed my heart and made me feel silly for ever feeling anxiety about meeting her.

She took my hand in hers and looked me right in my eyes and told me, *"He chose you in more ways than you can imagine. Because I can tell he loves you, and Yusuf's love lasts a lifetime."*

If that isn't the truth, nothing else is.

"Two large Americanos," the barista shouted my order this time.

I was heading to the counter when my phone chimed in my

pocket. Thinking it was just a simple little notification, I pulled my phone out of my pocket to glance at it. I blinked hard then brought my device's screen closer to my eyes to read the social handle and the message informing me the owner of the social handle tagged me in a post.

I froze in place.

"What the...?"

I immediately unlocked my device and tapped into the app to see what I thought I saw, my pulse racing so fast I could feel it in my damn neck.

"Oh my God."

It was a photo of me and Yusuf. He'd taken it with his professional camera the day we visited Prospect Park in Brooklyn. The leaves were an orange, brown, and yellow on the trees behind us, typical of early November. It was my favorite photo of us, something I told him when we took it.

We looked good. *Great.*

My only problem was he posted the picture on his damn social media page... the one he shared with his wife.

The one with the thousands of followers.

The one he shared with his wife!

"They're gonna rip me to pieces." I exhaled, releasing all the air in me. "Why would he post this here?!"

I rushed up to the counter, dropping my phone into my pocket, picking up the cups of coffees, already in coffee trays, and stormed toward the exit with plans to get my answer from the man himself.

* * *

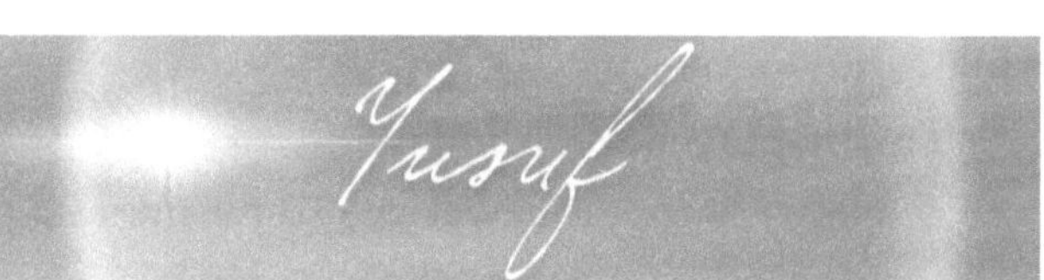

YUSUF

I placed my phone on the couch and got down on the floor to continue preparing for Clarke's arrival.

Knowing her, she got the notification and was flipping out.

I knew if I'd asked her first, she would've said no. Getting her to live beyond what she thinks she's capable of doing has been a challenge I love just as much as I loved her.

Thinking about that brought a smile to my face.

A year ago, I didn't think it was possible to experience this kind of love again. One that was exciting, fulfilling, and fed me in ways I'd been missing since having to say goodbye to my wife Parris.

Clarke was so good to me by her just being herself. Effervescent spitfire energy that was always fun trying to tame. But it was impossible. She was like a wild flower that grew in ways no one could control. I loved that so much about her.

Life after Maui took some getting used to. Being with Clarke made that easy.

Advised by my therapist, I took things slowly, as slow as I could before wanting *more* with Clarke.

I was a relationship kind of guy. I loved and thrived in partnerships. I enjoyed making Clarke happy and making her feel even better than she made me feel. So why delay? I was ready to build something with her and wanted to set the foundation for that from now.

So, we made things official. She introduced me to her family, and I introduced her to mine, and in the last six months, everything we have done has been meticulously executed to move us toward something solid.

Marriage.

I wouldn't ask her to marry me today.

Telling my followers about us was the step before that, though, and not for keeping total strangers in the loop of my love life.

I heard the raps at the hotel room door and stood to my feet to approach.

I'd booked the hotel room for the week for a staycation for the two of us.

We needed the break, and I knew I had plans to make the announcement about our relationship shortly after the new year. I needed a place that would make her happy.

She loved the view of Central Park in the winter, so I got a suite at a hotel with the perfect window view of the park.

"Yusuf," she voiced, wide eyed, as soon as I opened the door.

I smiled. "Hey beautiful."

"Don't you *hey beautiful* me."

"But you look so beautiful, babe."

She grunted and pushed past me to enter the suite. Clarke placed the tray of two coffees on the suite's kitchen counter and hurried on to removing her wool coat.

"Yusuf," she said again, approaching. "My love, what the hell is this?"

Clarke held up her phone, so the screen pointed at me. On it was the photo I posted to my socials, and that I tagged her in.

I focused on it for a few seconds, then told her, "New beginnings."

"New beginnings?!" she shrieked. "Yusuf, you posted a photo of you and your new girlfriend on the social account you shared with your wife. Do you know how bad this looks?"

"Some might feel that way," I answered with a nod. "But I didn't post it for them. Because if anyone looks at this picture of us and thinks anything negative, they were never for me or my happiness from the start."

She stared at me with wrinkle brows.

I walked up to her, moved her locs off her shoulders, smoothing them down her back.

"I posted it for the men and women like me who need a little slice of hope that there is life after loss."

Her eyes skated along the contours of my face, reading me.

"Come here." I threaded my fingers with hers and encouraged her to follow me to the living room.

I'd set up an indoor picnic on the blanket I spread over the hotel suite's carpet. Sandwiches, exotic fruit bowls, cheeses, and the expensive wine she loved so much in Hawaii that I found at a local wine store in New York.

On the TV was a video capturing the sunset at Haleakala National Park.

"Is that—"

"Our view?" I finished. "It is. I found a continuous loop of it online."

Her face lit up with a smile. "Oh, so you *knew* you were going to piss me off with that post, huh?"

I dropped my head to my chest to hold back my laugh, but it was impossible to.

Clarke made me laugh a lot, to the point of my face hurting. And I loved that change the most in my life.

I was genuinely happy these days and everyone could see it. My brother says it every time he sees me, and I sincerely feel it all over me.

There are days when I think of Parris, and it isn't a passing thought. I feel the heaviness in my heart that I have to breathe through to keep the tears from spilling from my eyes. But then I remember what Clarke told me on the beach after scattering Parris's ashes. Parris will always be with me for as long as I remembered her. And although my sadness from wishing Parris were still here, was an unpleasant one, I remembered her in those moments. She was alive in my heart. And with that knowledge, I knew to let the feeling pass because she wouldn't want me feeling anything but joy whenever she crossed my mind.

My therapist told me grief never really goes away. It just dulls in pain.

I was getting used to reflecting like a mirror all the good Clarke was to me. The mastery of that was something I enjoyed very much about our relationship.

Clarke leaned into my view. "Are you still with me here, space cadet?"

I laughed some more. "I'm here. I'm thinking about how to say this, so you understand and see no need to be pissed at me."

"I'm all ears."

"Parris and I," I started. "We lived a lot of our life on social media. And although I don't owe anybody *anything... they* didn't owe *me* anything, either. But they gave me a lot. They joined us on our journey and were there for the good times until the terrible. And they were there for me with supportive messages and posts that kept me strong when I didn't think I had any strength left in me. Complete strangers were praying for me, Clarke, and I never took that for granted. I never thought I'd want to update any of my accounts ever again, but... you changed all of that for me."

Her face softened.

"Parris and I wanted to show our love in all facets that our love represented and..." I shrugged. "I wanted to show the people who loved and followed us from the beginning what happened next after her sudden passing. So, I told them, and I showed them the woman I feel saved my life. Because before you, Clarke," I said, taking her face into my hand, "I thought I'd never be happy again. Love was never in my plans after Parris. It wasn't even a thought. But I wanted happiness again, and I didn't see how I ever could have it much less *be* it... until I met *you*."

Her shoulders relaxed as she exhaled and settled into the suite's couch cushions.

"I should've asked you first, but I knew you'd say no. I knew it might upset you when I did it, but that was the risk I was willing to take to feed two birds with one seed." I smiled. "I wanted... no, I *needed* to show you immense gratitude for your existence, and I wanted to show them the beautiful thing that occurs when life gives you sunsets... the ones you *never* wanted to see or believed you could ever love."

She smiled, eyes watering as always. "What happens?"

"It gets dark after." I swallowed hard. "So dark, you believe the light is gone forever. But then you realize that only in the dark can you see how beautiful life truly is, much like how only when the sky is dark can you see the stars shine the brightest. And just like night, darkness has to end, which means the dawn is never as far away as we think."

Tears fell from her eyes, and I caught them both with my thumb.

"You're my star and my dawn, Clarke. A dawn I cherish beyond the physical and that I never thought I'd ever get again after all that darkness. And I just..." I exhaled through my lips. "I just wanted the people who sincerely cared for Parris and me, to know I'm more than all right. I'm great. I'm not exactly the same. I've had to change, and that's okay. And people going through what I had to go through will be okay, too."

Clarke placed a hand against my chest.

"If you want me to take it down, though, I will." I picked up my phone. "But I read a few of the comments after posting the photo and the people had nothing but kind things to say... and they think you're finer than wine."

She arched both brows. "They commented that?"

"*Mm-hmm.*" I shrugged. "They commented you were fine. I added the wine part."

She grinned. "Well, if they think I'm *fine*, I guess it can stay up."

I hollered a laugh. "It'll be my last post on there. I mentioned that in the caption with the rest of what I've just told you. I just wanted them to know what life is like on the other side of loss and that their guy is okay and being taken great care of."

Clarke reached over and wrapped her arms around the back of my neck, pressing her lips to mine.

"I love you, Yusuf."

I rested my forehead against hers and said, "And I love you, too, Clarke."

We pressed our lips to one another and moaned at the feel of us on each other.

This never got old. Her in my space and me in hers. It was the start to something so beautiful. I could feel it deep in me.

She broke our kiss to say, "I see my favorite wine is in attendance."

"*Mm-hmm.*" I licked my lips and used my thumb to clean beneath her bottom lip. "Shall we?"

"We shall." She smiled. "We can have the coffee later."

I uncorked the bottle and poured out the rich wine into both of our glasses. Handed hers to her.

Clarke held her glass in the air and said, "To sunsets."

"To sunsets," I echoed, nodding slowly while lifting my glass to clink with hers. "May they remind us that endings can be beautiful too."

THE END.

Dear Reader,

Thank you for reading *When Life Gives You Sunsets*. I hope you enjoyed reading it as much as I enjoyed creating it.

I love characters who challenge me. Characters who, at the start of their story, it almost seems impossible for me to pen a realistic happily ever after for them. Although I've written characters like Clarke many times before, I have never written a character like Yusuf.

Yusuf is one of my favorite male characters. These new male characters that keep finding me and are in touch with their feelings are quickly becoming some of my new favorites. Though I haven't experienced what Yusuf has experienced, I feel things deeply. So, when I got the idea of writing a story involving his character and his present circumstances, my heart ached for him the more and more I developed his character. Here's a man who truly loved his wife, knew she was the one at an age that everyone believed he was too young to know for sure. But he did, and his wife and he had many years and to him they weren't enough. He imagined what it would be like to grow old with her. He wanted to grow old with her! A man who welcomed the natural changes in life but was unprepared to deal with the end.

So, I knew when I wrote his story, I could not half-ass it. I could not write his story like any other story I've written because his experience was unique. Even his intimate scenes were an extension of his grief. I knew I needed to illustrate his tug of war between his loyalty and refusal to let go and his desire to feel everything but sad anymore, which would require him to love himself enough to move on without his wife. As he said, he felt his grief was threaded in his new identity, and it was important to show that. It was important to show that even in paradise, someone could feel like hell in it.

While I've penned characters like Clarke in similar circumstances, it was a lot of fun working with hers. Clarke is the type of person to swear they're ready for things but really aren't.

I can relate lol.

Throughout the story, it was important to show this in her actions and reactions, starting with her line, I included in the epigraph, from book one, *When Luke Met Juliette*. She said an innocent indirect prayer and actually got what she wanted, but she wasn't really ready for the gravity of it all, considering she was on vacay and Yusuf was grieving the death of his wife. She said she wanted Freaknik lol but froze at the sight of Yusuf in the nude! And we kept on getting these moments of *I want this, but do I?* from Clarke until the very end, only now she realizes that the challenges and stepping out of her comfort zone also aids in her growth. Like Nana pointed out, you cannot choose how life gifts you. Those gifts may not look like gifts at all. And Clarke finally learned how to accept and unwrap hers.

I really love that for her. And I love that for them.

These two needed each other at a time they thought they didn't. And more than a romance, this story was life analyzed, which you should already know by now is my favorite song.

Clarke's lesson was to live the life she wants to love, and Yusuf's lesson was to live the life he still has. And I think these two are well on their ways of mastering their given lessons.

Last year, I made it a goal to pen a vacation novel. I'd never done it and really wanted to. I'm so happy *When Life Gives You Sunsets* was the story I told.

I'm going to miss these two. Hopefully, in the future, we can catch up with them again.

Before penning this story, I would have never imagined the devastation that swept through Maui because of wildfires in early August 2023. Hawaii is and will always be one of my favorite places on earth and I pray with words and actions the people of Hawaii can recover, restore, and rebuild. Bigger than the island, it is the people who make that place feel like home. Maui was the unofficial third character in this story and she has a special place in my heart.

Thank you so much for reading. I hope you enjoyed *When Life Gives You Sunsets* as much as I enjoyed writing it.

If this is your first story you've read by me and you enjoyed it, welcome! You're what I like to call a Brookelynite now.

If you've been reading from a book or many books ago, I thank you so much for reading yet another story from my catalog. I am humbled by every book release because of your continued support!

My aim is always to keep this journey interesting for us both. All these books later and you're still here?!

That's dope.

That's amazing.

That's love!

Thank you.

See you at the end of the next book!

Love,
BK.

character cameos

In the order they appeared or were mentioned in When Life Gives You Sunsets...

Esme
When Luke Met Juliette

Rylee Daniels
Last Comes Love
Ready or Not

Lennox Walker
Last Comes Love

Juliette
When Luke Met Juliette

Luke
When Luke Met Juliette

Maurice

Lena's Ex-File

book club questions

1. What was your first impression of Clarke?

2. What was your first impression of Yusuf?

3. What did you think of the way Clarke and Yusuf met?

4. What are your thoughts on Yusuf's loyalty to his late wife?

5. Do you think Clarke was wrong about pursuing Yusuf, considering Yusuf was still grieving?

6. What would you have done if you were Clarke and you fell for someone like Yusuf?

7. What was your favorite moment from When Life Gives You Sunsets?

8. What was the most valuable takeaway from *When Life Gives You Sunsets* according to you?

9.   What did you think about the ending?

10. What did you love the very most about *When Life Gives You Sunsets*?

Brookelyn wrote her first short story when she was a sophomore in high school. Back then she discovered how using her experience as a teen living in Brooklyn to create romantic shorts was just as exciting to her as retail shopping and going on dates. After starting her first semester of college two years later, Brookelyn's creative writing became more of a hobby and something to escape the stress of midterms and finals.

Now in her 30s as a freelance writer, penning short stories and novellas is her everything. While her experience with writing has evolved for the better, her undying love for creating fiction remains unchanged. Brookelyn's focus is on creating contemporary women's fiction with characters based in urban settings. Her stories chronicle the emotional journeys and erotic experiences of women today through her characters and the scenarios they're thrown into.

The motivation behind her brand of writing has a lot to do with what she discovered storytelling provided for her - an escape. Her goal with her work is to create characters and urban worlds that offer a great escape for fiction readers looking for a break from the daily grind of adulting and who prefer to relax with good books and short stories.

When she's not freelance copywriting, doing yoga, or showing her husband, son, and daughter lots of love, she can be found sitting at her computer desk, with her legs folded, and a cup of coffee (or a glass of wine) at arm's reach as she types or edits her latest short or novella.

Connect With Me Online!

Twitter: @brookelynmosley
Facebook: http://facebook.com/brookelynmosley
Facebook Reading Group: Brookelynites Book Lounge
Instagram: @Brookelynmosley
My Website: BrookelynMosley.com
My Readers Website: BKBookLounge.com
My Mailing List: BK Insiders (*Sign up at BrookelynMosley.com and receive 4 complimentary shorts in your email when you sign up as a new subscriber!*)